THE LOST THOUGHTS
OF SOLDIERS

THE LOST THOUGHTS
OF SOLDIERS

DELIA FALCONER

COUNTERPOINT | BERKELEY

Library of Congress Cataloging-in-Publication Data

Falconer, Delia, 1966-
    The lost thoughts of soldiers / by Delia Falconer.
        p. cm.
    ISBN: 978-1-58243-528-2
1. Benteen, Frederick William, 1834-1898—Fiction. 2. Little Bighorn, Battle of the, Mont., 1876—Fiction. I. Title

PR9619.3.F287L67 2006
823'.914—dc22

                                                    2009025608

Cover design by Gopa & Ted2
Printed in the United States of America

COUNTERPOINT
2117 Fourth Street
Suite D
Berkeley, CA 94710

www.counterpointpress.com

Distributed by Publishers Group West

10 9 8 7 6 5 4 3 2 1

FOR RICHARD, AS ALWAYS—
AND SIMEON

We saw the Zeppelin above us, just ahead, amid a gleaming of clouds: high up, like a bright golden finger, quite small, among a fragile incandescence of clouds. And underneath it were splashes of fire as the shells fired from the earth burst. Then there were flashes near the ground—and the shaking noise. It was like Milton—"then there was war in heaven." But it was not angels. It was the small golden Zeppelin, like a long oval world, high up. It seemed as if the cosmic order were gone, as if there had come a new order, a new heaven above us. I cannot get over it, that the moon is not queen of the sky by night . . . So it is the end—our world is gone, and we are like dust in the air.

D. H. Lawrence

THE LOST THOUGHTS
OF SOLDIERS

He moves indirectly.

At dawn, before he can get to the shaving mirror, he is standing here in the kitchen in his undershirt, the wet brush in his hand.

Odd paths his feet take these days, following creases in the daylight. Heading out to shred his pipe plug on the doorstep, he finds himself in the study, staring at the leaning spines of books. He stands by doors and feels the handles. He spends half-days at the windows, his hands in his pockets, his hips against the sills.

There is a slow brown river at the bottom of the garden. For two hours yesterday he watched it, in the middle of the afternoon, when he had intended to close the shutters and take his nap. His wife found him, shoeless, sitting on the landing. Small drops of rain in the dull grey heat around them. An electric hiss on the water's surface. The smell of soil and green things washing from the edges. He took Frabbie's hand and made her lean down to feel the cool airspace, rising, that formed beneath his feet.

The quiet drift of flour to the table. A strange calm at sunrise that he associates with armies.

Lathered up, his braces hanging from his waist, he stands against the kitchen doorway. The maid slaps the bottom of the sieve and stirs the sausage gravy, pretending not to see.

Indoors he can feel the river turning over.

The fronts of houses here are blank, the real life centered around the muscle of the water. The town is an afterthought, its main street beginning a quarter-mile from his front door.

His father built this house here, in Georgia, on the river-bank, and named his home "The Shadows." Ten rooms, thick walls, cold flagstones on the veranda. There are wet hydrangeas beneath the windows, watered already by the staff.

When he was a boy his father showed him on a map how neatly these plantations lined themselves up along the river. A surprise how their straight edges gridded outwards from the banks, since he had only learned the shaded lanes which wound between them. These roads take unpredictable jinks, turn suddenly catty-corner towards the water and loop back, someone told him, because the surveyors who planned them had been drunk. They laid them down through the bone orchards, the cemeteries of the poor. Fragments of collarbone and femur still rise up sometimes, bleached and glowing, after heavy rains.

Often the poor were buried with their silver. That was an unforgettable sound of his childhood, the percussion against carriage wheels of a tarnished candlestick or fork.

Stale pain on his breath—and, he suspects, a more feral stink about the groin. His bladder aches, his skin is goosebumped.

He thinks, I must cellar my body here like rotting fruit.

He has installed a small water closet in his study, behind a screen, so that he does not have to haul himself upstairs as often to the bedroom. He opens the study door and sees the husky outline of his desk, the dull shapes of handguns lined up along the top shelf of a bookcase. Mold and coal-dust in the closed-up air. There are thin bright lines across the window, but he does not open it, he wants to feel shapeless a little longer.

The urge to urinate is constant, the results are always paltry. Lately he has taken to carrying the pan out through the back door to the rose beds, watching the ants run when he pours his trickle on the damp soil near the roots. In New York, in a dark cathedral entrance, an old nun once sold him candy. She told him how the medieval monks would piss in the stained glass when it was molten to produce the creamy yellow. That one thought changed the whole of Europe for him. She had mimed it, leaning backwards, the invisible cock in one clawed hand. Her old eyes were bright, but not salacious. He recognized her as a young girl in a farmyard. He feels a cousin pleasure here, in the thought of his own sluggish fluids emerging perfumed and phosphorescent in those canary-yellow blooms.

He sleeps naked these nights beside his wife, his body as white as those a flood or warfare leave.

His mind also wanders. His life a set of dark rooms which he moves through. Some things he remembers, others he seems to have imagined.

One night in winter, many years ago, when they were tenting in Nebraska, Frabbie wanted him to wake and touch her. So she took an icy handful of lead shot and dropped it in his lap.

✎

He hears muffled birdsong through the window and knows the sky has broken. A shift in the day, like religion starting. You can only feel it later, you cannot spot where it begins.

At the far end of the garden the ducks run up to greet him. They look like feathered lizards; he likes the meanness of their reptile eyes, those scaly legs. Beyond the beds of flowers and the benches they have made this section of the lawn a quag-mire—there are musky droppings and feathers churned up with the thick dark mud. A hint of phlegm that reminds him of the floors of bars so rank with throat oysters that if you leaned forward to tie your shoelace it could nearly make you faint. The female has hatched six ducklings. They skim madly across the water, away from her, then reconverge; darting at sharp angles, as swift as marbles on an ice rink.

For a while he measures time in breadcrumbs.

He has the dim feeling this may be a church day. No groundsman in the yard, hurried bangs and clatters from the kitchen. The air is tense with the metallic sense of bells anticipating. The birds seem less eager for the bread, as if they know they will soon feast on the wedding rice that floats downstream from the town.

Yesterday, when he had finished shaving in the study, the lather had gone lardy, and he'd had to wet and scrape it with his nails, as if he had botched his death mask. He keeps a kit in there, behind the curtain, in the same way that he has the second water closet, or hides the extra matches on tabletops and ledges in the house. He hopes he does not end up like the old people he sees parked out on verandas, on divans, nodding in the sunlight; who appear in the backgrounds of photographs, their jaws a blur, as if they chew imaginary bacon. There is a grim pleasure, though, in imagining the future: Lamps and candles forbidden by his son. The names of friends in his pockets on little scraps of paper. Notes on the piano from his wife, reminding him to bathe.

Two crows as sleek as big black cats linger on the edges of the quacking, and take it in turns to hop in with pointed ease to steal a mouthful. He throws a crust to a drake that has lost a foot to a trapper or a fish.

Since those two days pinned down on the ridge at Little Bighorn he has been able to feel his own life, and that is no good thing. Sometimes it floats like a shadowy cast before his eyes, filling and unfilling like a curtain. Sometimes it is a high, ecstatic whistling in his head, like the wind on those grass hills that leaped into their mouths and scrubbed out the hollows of their skulls. At other times, like now, it is a sad and solitary thing, no bigger than a mouse or frog, a timid weight.

His slippers are black and unsaveable, he guesses.

But he is safe, within the grey heart of the morning.

Last night, pressed against his wife's back, he dreamed of a field of daffodils, each filled to the brim with piss.

⤝⤞

There is a weight in the sunlight now across his shoulders.

The sounds of a carriage on the road.

The odor of coffee, like the spunky whiff of some secret body fluid, finds him, as it unwinds across the grass. Always, it has been this smell that lets him know he is alive, the steam moistening his chin, the hot cup between his hands. Out on the plains when the men were frozen and bone-weary they would sometimes rest their heads sideways on their mugs, to imagine the hot breath of wives and lovers in their ears.

He detours past the kitchen garden and the rose beds to

the ice house; past the ghost garden, a bed of pale grey lambs' tongues and silver creepers that grow in the shade provided by the house.

Inside, he sees nothing at first but blackness and the vapor of his breath. Vegetables and flesh in hibernation in the pit below him. He hears tiny fissures open in the ice like the infinitesimal and random tickings of little pocket watches. Maggots sound similar, he recalls—a more liquidy eagerness about the ticking as they burrow through a corpse.

The ice is cut in January, when it is thickest, from frozen ponds in New England, and packed in sawdust and transported southwards in the train. Sometimes, when it is delivered, he will stand by the back of the cart and brush the chaff from the wet surface of the blocks. It is often possible to see a pale silver fish or water-skimming insect suspended beneath the surface, some creature deficient in suspicious instincts, surprised by the swiftness with which the water froze.

He had almost forgotten the woman.

The night before the fighting, in the cold dark, she had slipped as quiet as a ghost out of the cottonwoods' brown shadow. Her face when she asked them for some dollars was untouchable and grave. She led and they had followed, a dozen of them, Custer, Young Tom, himself, the officers Star-Gazer and Handsome Jack, some of the enlisted men, down to the Rosebud's banks. Their footsteps Indian quiet. The same bright mercury in their chests as they felt before a charge. Glancing sidelong at each other's eyes to see dog appetite and fear.

How vast it was and black, that untelegraphed land. Her straight back electric in a white cotton dress.

Did the others also feel it on nights like this—the sudden longing to see their sperm spill like silver coins across the ground?

She stopped at the river, which they smelled but could not see just then since there was no moon. Only the feeling that they had reached the edge where the land broke, its wet seam, the movement of chill water from high mountains. They shivered, although the air around them still held the terrible stillness of the day.

When the clouds passed they saw that she had left her dress on the bank, folded as if to make a gift around her boots. She floated on her back, the river halfway up her chest, as if asleep. Their throats ached with the beauty of it. Her white skin. The soft movement of the fur down there. A small hand just breaking the surface like a turtle's back.

The moon took another spell and she was gone.

Later, in spite of his tiredness, he would lie beneath his blanket with his eyes closed, imagining her cold breast, and direct his own hot gush across his hand.

The dining room door is open, the shutters thrown back, the silver on the table as he passes. A stack of napkins on the sideboard, not yet folded and laid out beside the plates. Some ruffled, no longer deadpan feeling, suddenly, about these hollow rooms on either side of the corridor. The humid air that has followed him through the back door lingers for a moment at the entrance to the study, then retreats.

When he was discharged he bought himself this armchair for the study, which he sits in now, the plushest and deepest he could find. It is true, that old soldiers' tale that years of riding shake the stuffing from you. This morning he feels as if he has just dismounted. His medicine bottles, made of muddy brown glass, are lined up before him on the table. He uses them as paperweights. Filled with liquids to different heights, they hold down old route maps, newspapers, unanswered correspondence, thin account books. *Raleigh, Vaughan, Swannanoa*—he can sit for hours feeling the names of places in high raised letters on the glass.

He takes a draught of something astringent from a bottle and leans back. Which is for the inside or the outside, guesswork sometimes. The alcohol whiff on his fingers when he caps it.

A bar in Texas which the locals called "Snake Nation." There was a regular there who would call you over, ask if you wanted to see his baby rabbit, then open up his jacket. Beneath his heart, the liver was voluptuous and swollen, quivering, as if some shy animal breathed beneath the tight, white skin.

In the bedroom above, he hears his wife Frabbie's steps. Sure movements—she does not pause, as he does when his feet first hit the floorboards, to gauge the weight of morning. Six quick paces to the water closet, the muffled sounds of dressing. She will leave it for the maid to throw the bedroom shutters open. She will not linger in her nightdress at the window. There will be a brief stop at the mirror, no vanity about her.

She walks swiftly, at the center of her slippers.

The difference in footsteps. Some organ in the body of tiny registrations. In the army, on the night watch, he could instantly sense a set of "cool steps," the term he used to think of them—the approach of unknown feet.

The first time he asked Frabbie for a dance she had snatched at his hands, the way spinsters grab a cat or baby, as if they want to pull its love up by the roots. Something in that eagerness which moved him. Her broad back beneath his palm, lean thighs against his own. She held his arm tight as they stepped together, her thumb tucked in the firm groove of his muscles. The thrill of her finger there between the tendons each time he turned her in the waltz.

He feels his tailbone press against the cushions. Relentless riding severs old connections and reroutes them: the discretion of soft organs, the heart's place in the chest, are all disrupted. Instead, new avenues for pain develop. Tailbone might connect to kneebone, sternum to rectum, hand to thigh.

There is a rosebud on his desk, pale pink, the head still beaded, that he has brought in for her from the garden. The carriage clock, Chinese vase, framed portraits, are still part of the mantel's bulk in these last moments of the half-light.

Soon, he thinks, all these things will be antiques.

He takes the opener from its sheath and begins to sort the letters. Some are old, and brittle from being left in his study since the winter, the paper thinned and dried out by the fire. He splits the envelopes cleanly, although his hands are shaking. He feels their corners in the soft flesh of his palm.

A year afterward, in their honeymoon bed, both virgins, she squeezed his cock in her long dry fingers. Both saw the small hole open, both heard the tiny click.

There is a self-centered inward-turning quality about this time of year. Things draw the steam in, expanding on their essence. In two days the slippers he has shucked off this morning at the doorstep and aligned neatly side by side beneath the scraper will be as moldy as pumpkins. If he leaves the bottle uncapped before he goes to bed he will find small green clots like duckweed on the surface of his ink.

A strange, aggressive softness.

He unfolds the sheets of paper, spreads them out.

Twenty years after that whole grief show and they still chase the corpse of Custer. He shuffles through the letters— a retired West Pointer, he can tell by the high military loops of careful copperplate; a doctor's scrawl, the headlong green ink of a madman. Some enclose long monographs, hoping for corrections. Others, crosses and lines on ornate maps. Some ask for nothing, but these he finds the most disturbing, as if they extract some shapeless promise from him. They send him clippings from the newspapers, where they advance their theories on the battle. Underlinings in thick pencil, long column-inches folded around their cards.

Why is it that only men write? After all, if an opinion is on the menu he has never known a woman to refuse it. But there is more than argument, he thinks, in these frail pages.

The shy atheism of the male. He remembers from the army. A touching need to find their gods in one another on this earth.

>==<

He hears voices on the street beyond the window, filtered through warm church-light. A shift in bird-life towards the workmen's noises; he feels swift shadows touch the shutters, hears the feathered concentration in cool places. The water cart damps down the road before the bells begin.

He will not oblige them, the eager boy or retired West Pointer, by going over the details of the fight. He will not reread and comment on his own testimony, describe the dust clouds, examine the cartridge shells that they have sent him. He will not go point by point through their numbered lists. Instead, he will write back as their "friend" and thank them for their kindness. He is out of that whirlpool now.

War is nine-tenths nothing, he wants to say.

And now, behind him, there is the sense of skirts, a well-bound corset, layers of thick warm air and softness underneath. A kiss on his silver skull-top. He tilts his head back until it finds Frabbie's solid hip.

She looks at his desk and says it is a start.

He holds her hand against his cheek and pats her forearm. They seldom stroke each other's flesh now, he notices, something to do with growing older. Like the other couples he sees around the main street, gently slapping backs and shoulders. As if there is no frisky sap beneath the skin, as if the nerves of love have passed the stage of ripeness. The soft contempt of married life.

She tells him he should come soon, she can smell the coffee burning. That old familiar pepper in her steps as she heads out to supervise the maid.

I'll be there momentarily, he says.

He has never wanted another woman. That whole worry about whether it's done right.

In a chest upstairs, packed away in tissue and camphor, his old military jacket with his brevet rank that she will lay him out in. It is dark and heavy, a hint of grog and horsehair still about the lining. After a drunk, he would lie on his bed with it on his face, cool as coffin silk, and fill it with his breath. Sour caper juice in his throat, ready for ignition. His own ghost shape in the sleeves and the thick curve of the shoulders. Talking to Star-Gazer and the others out there somewhere in the blackness.

The art of drinking: You've got to know how to fall, he used to say, kick free of the stirrups before the ground breaks in two beneath you.

Once, before the years of snow and drink and failure brought these sharp spasms to his bladder, he could go into a mad rut just to see the inside of Frabbie's wrist.

A dream he had, three nights after the clean-up from the battle, of Captain Keogh, dead, undressing in her room.

That same feeling each morning nowadays, of a second close and silky dark around his head, when he first wakes.

He folds his thin silver glasses and puts them on the table. With the heel of his hand he stretches out his eye flesh. He must sort through his papers soon, his promise to her.

From the other side of the river, faintly, he hears a pack of dogs fight. A last high yelp which is percussive, even joyful. He suspects they have found some injured water creature or foul meat in a trap. At the other end of the house Frabbie and the maid talk softly. A smell of biscuits enters from the hallway, chairs scrape, the bookshelf has sharp edges. The air around him is unseamed now and clear.

And here, on the desk before him, is his whole biography, pinched into those two days at Little Bighorn. The name he forgets to think of himself by, sometimes, *Frederick Benteen*. The man who let Custer die. Who was not half the solider.

The morning hardens.

He feels his life settle and grow solid like the light.

LATELY, HE HEARS THEM ALL THE TIME:

Star-Gazer, named because he wore glasses.

Handsome Jack, who leaned in and stroked his horse's dick as he was speaking, who lay on his back on his bedroll and composed his lists of farts.

Star-Gazer pushes his glasses up his nose with his small hand. I have a dog that eats mice, he says, his face deadpan. I had a depression once which I cured by eating shellfish.

There is a gentle sweetness in Handsome Jack's face as he leans suddenly with his whisky across the campfire to whisper in your ear, Do you want a punch in the cunt?

Others who exist only in a sentence.

Pritzker, who told him of a dream he had once of carrying a sack of cats out to the desert and teaching them to paint.

Monroe, the cowboy. He did not like cows because of all the skull inside their faces.

The bugler, De Rudio, who practiced saying *wool* and *wolf*.

Bender who called out Bartender, oh bartender! whenever they were getting close to camp.

It is Handsome Jack who plies Sully the enlisted man with grog; who whoops each time the man makes his grave pronouncement, Nature is a slut.

At first he suspects the boy's letter is from the crazed brigade that writes to him in gaudy inks.

The dead are liars, it begins. *We are both acquainted with that knowledge.*

> *I approach you, Sir, as a Man of Action, assuming that, like myself, you are no great fan of the philosophies of the stoic, Epicetus. (Although given your exposure to the "core of things" I should be greatly interested in your reading of the Greeks.)*

The packet is postmarked from a suburb in Chicago. There is something hard left inside it, folded in a handkerchief which slides from the pile of papers where he props it to the floor.

> *It may surprise you to receive correspondence from one so young who lives at such a distance. While it is true that I have not yet gained my nineteenth year I*

have spent much of my life, as they say, "in books."
I have employment at this time with a stationery
company in the city of Chicago where I find I am by
nature impelled to quibble with the records. It is my
fervent wish that I may argue your case against the
malicious ghost of Custer and those who would claim
him as a hero.

This boy believes that Benteen *saved the men's bacon, as
it were,* at Little Bighorn by leading the rest of the troops
toward that ridge, in spite of the *concerted attempt* by Custer
to have them join him in the grave.

The letter continues for five pages, filled with the
pompous longing of young men.

While enjoying an existence of humble anonymity at
present, the boy concludes, he rather flatters himself—but
not without some cause, he hopes—that he will become a
rather familiar name around the hearthsides of the nation
upon publication of his *controversial volume* on the Battle.
He looks forward to their working together to restore
Benteen's reputation.

He signs himself, *with enormous admiration*, Nathan
Brodhead, (Senior) Clerk.

The carte-de-visite, a studio portrait, Benteen guesses has
been taken after work—a limp graininess about the collar,
moist pawprints on the book the boy clutches upright on his

lap as if he holds a baby on his knees. He has that Irish type of eye, round and eerie and brimful. Something German in the pale moustache and sideburns. And the transparent look about the chops of a man who lives on vegetables alone. He wants the photographer to like him, sitting stiff and upright. A crier, Benteen supposes, he could always pick them in the army, the sense of some secret wound beneath the collar-bone, the upper lip too full and soft.

A ginger hair rears up from the starchy handkerchief which held the photograph.

He has not passed through the door yet, Benteen thinks.

Like the faint stirrings of sex, he feels old venom sacks filling; the swelling weight of another, second, body within the old made up of bitter organs.

So. This is his avenger.

He pictures him cooking beans in a small room in a boarding house that is overrun with cats.

I joined the army to write poems, that is what Star-Gazer says.

This is enough to shut up even Custer, and Young Tom, who is about to put a pair of queens down on the table.

The same quick silence that comes sometimes with a fall

of snow outside; someone strikes a match and you can hear the separate, soft ignitions of tobacco and of paper. Custer was halfway though another of his glory tales—seeming to look inward, then glancing up to see if you could also feel God passing. Now, except for those restless hands that seem always to be tallying something, or working out how it would feel if it was opened up, he is quite still. One of the hounds jerks its head up from his knee.

Star-Gazer, on the bench beside the window, sits there with his legs crossed. He has a thick overlip. His thin shoulders stoop. He looks out at the Kansas twilight.

But what I learned quickly, he says, is that I cannot rhyme for money—so I'm working on a novel now instead.

Impossible, as always, to tell if he is pulling all their legs or drawing on some dark and limpid source of information.

Next Handsome Jack, who has been sitting in the corner, yawns and stretches. His drinking face is on, perversely calm, mysterious with juice. He says he joined up for precisely the same reason. I am a swiver for the sonnet, a dibbler for a ditty, a biter for a ballad, Handsome Jack says. Oh I'm a moaner for a metaphor, he adds.

A kind of act the two men have between them.

As he looks back, Benteen wonders if there might have been more to it.

In the fireplace the knothole in a log cracks. Young Tom tells his brother Custer, whom he calls Big Dog, that he had better pony up.

The light behind Star-Gazer is liqourish and pale. His lenses, when he turns to face them, are bright and filled with blankness.

I like sonnets, he says.

After the battle, among the mud and scraps of men, he would find Star-Gazer's notebooks.

Bits of their conversations taken down in his crabbed hand. Quotations cut from books and stuck down in the center of the pages.

Attempts at calculation scribbled in the dark.

What is a life worth?
5 ducks.
800 horses.
1 skull (Indian)—$1.50

A note on himself, Benteen:

B. Fears the ocean. Says all things joined to other things.

How many types of nakedness are there, Benteen wonders now.

Standing in the street, outside their wall, he watches Frabbie heading for the church.

At breakfast she took her coffee in small sips. In her mind she already had her hat on, her back against the straight oak of the pew. At each swallow, a muscle kicked like a small frog inside her neck. She has never gone to church for God, she says, but for the way it layers out the silence.

A bee worries at the grass beside his feet, as if there is not enough warmth or color for it in this morning. For the moment he is his daylight self. The pomade on his hair has dried in ridges, his coat is clean and brushed.

At breakfast Frabbie put a piece of bacon on his plate. She did not speak. The same courtesy she showed to the children, the four dead, and Freddie who lives and who they fear for, still; a way she had of smoothing a ribbon on a smock and sitting back, as if allowing them the choice of being a baby or some other, more magnificent, thing that they might think of.

He watches the doctor on his way to some birthing or unbirthing, the quiet widow, the silent negroes heading to their own churches, the seller of grain talking to his horse. The streets are filled with habit and still shadow.

When he first brought her roses she put them by the tight heads into a vase which she carried to her sisters' room. She had never had a dream of being rescued. She had not expected, she once told him, to be either joyful or unhappy.

And now the old men come, the dog-like wanderers of

morning, who recognize each other, stop and sniff and lift their tails up at this at once sad and frisky hour, on their way to sun themselves on verandas. They pause to greet him. Has he found a new mare yet? Will Frabbie come to the cake sale? How is his health this morning?

His place in town. As some grave, stiff symbol of endurance. He thinks of the cold-jawed lions in San Marco that someone once told him of, which the children sit on, which the tourists dress in fancy hats.

When he asked her, she stepped into their marriage without pausing. He thinks of it as his one brave moment. The same sensation of grace he had sometimes when he used to fish—the step forward, the question thrown out simple as a reflex, and there, heavy and surprising, was her life.

Not yet, he says. It is probable. Fair to middling, he answers.

He wants to reply to these old men. How once in a Chinatown somewhere he saw a woman standing in a doorway, a sharp knife poised at a perfect angle in a peach. That some trees are filled with birds and others empty. That he passed a turd this morning, half-bent from all the sitting, and thought of Handsome Jack.

For how long did he hope for such a letter?

Years afterward, if someone recognized him in a bar, he would refuse to shake their hand. I am Benteen's ghost, he'd say, and liquor up.

A dawning sense that he had wasted his life chasing the wrong ending, that the only thing to do was throw more waste on top.

Not straight afterward, but years on, it seemed that history had fallen out in pictures—a change that cur had bet on somehow. The long hair, the way he colored out the horses; the way he moved, as if his path was tungsten-lit. As if he shouted, On, you wolverines!—not to the troops, but to the biographers he could hear already licking at their chops.

For some years he could not help talking of it. It's not the drink, but history, he'd say, to anyone who sat beside him on a drunk.

This is what the boy should know, he thinks.

I have never had the grease to be a hero: the spring in the walk, the chest that moves beneath the weight of medals not yet won. I have always moved like this, the invisible dog snapping at my heels.

No bright path has ever opened up before me.

Strange, the first thing he thought of when he heard that Handsome Jack had also been among the dead.

They had been tenting for three weeks in Wyoming around the Platte's north fork. Wolfing it, for the most part, killing what they could to make up for the hard tack. Sometimes they heard the ripe sounds of trout and frogs leaping in the river. They felt the damp eyes of elk and deer at some unspecified proximity around them in the darkness.

In that night they undid their bedrolls.

Damn, I've been shitted! Handsome Jack called out.

Benteen lit a taper from the fire coals.

They saw Handsome Jack peering at a turd of awesome scale that had been rolled up in his mattress. A punishment, no doubt, for the last weeks of complaint about the lack of fibrous powers in the food, for his endless talk and lists of defecation.

Star-Gazer reached for his spectacles.

Jesus. I would be proud of that myself, he said.

At first Handsome Jack believed that it was Custer. They had to stop him going over to his tent where he said he would crush his chinless head between two Bibles. Then he decided on the cook—or Young Tom, whose ugly phiz he could picture bearing down on such a jewel. He threatened, to be sure of his revenge, that he would slip it in the cooking pot before the morning, or something just as good.

At last a suspect calm spread itself across his face. That

look he had sometimes, like a pasty angel. He sat still for a while as if he listened for the first strains of a pious concert.

To make it worse, he said at last, I think I now have lupabrilles.

His look alarmed them, they did not speak.

Lupabrilles were hemorrhoids so long, he explained, that they hung down from the anus—they made a high-pitched squeaking sound each time you walked. Like this, he said, and made the little *eek eek* noises with his mouth.

He clenched his buttocks and minced with a swift nimbleness toward the river.

They could still hear his soft squeaking, and his laughter, as he reached the far edge of camp.

Impossible then to imagine Handsome Jack as he would become those last few months before the battle. His face surly as they rode at night into the cold north wind, his hat pulled low, a sallow grievance nursed within his beard. The horses stumbling in pale ravines which opened in the moonlight. He would only grunt when Benteen rode up, abreast, to speak.

Surrounding himself instead with that group of losers and enlisted men he referred to as "the Choir."

Sully, the Chimpanzee. Ambrose the Bilk, Burton the Whale, Marshall known as Moony. Burkman, in charge of Custer's dogs, who collected scraps and minced them for the puppies. Scruggs who had been given Death Valley from the first day as his mount.

That bore, Maybliss.

Simms who did backflips for no reason.

To each, as they brought him their troubles, Handsome Jack would incline his head and nod gravely like a pope. He would listen to their philosophies with a look of holy wonder.

It was Young Tom who had said something about them, one afternoon, when they had stopped to rest the horses. Handsome Jack looked past the Choir towards the plains as he squatted in the sagebrush, as if he imagined their silhouettes against a different background. He would not meet Young Tom's eyes.

They are the ones who *know*, is all he said.

Benteen thinks of the photograph again.

And in his mind, suddenly, he sees the boy standing at the counter of a shop with ink-stained hands, mooning over lunch meats. Or hunched over at the opera with a bag of popcorn squeezed between his knees.

He feels it again, the perverse pleasure that used to come to him when drinking hard, at the thought of signing his life over to this wet-dick.

His hatred is voluptuous all these years on.

He thinks of how to begin his story for the boy.

Death found me, not on the battlefield where I was pre-pared to meet it as a gentleman, but buried me with paper and with words.

He stops. He hears, as he has always done throughout his life, this voice of his he barely recognizes. Ghosting around the edges of its own self. Never one of those who step into their lives as if they simply put a set of clothes on.

Like Custer and that wife of his, who seemed to live on the outsides of their skins. Or simple, stout De Rudio the bugler, whom he watched as he invented tunes, his brow creased, the air and thoughts combining deep within his belly. Who said to him once, in that pleased German way of his, "I am *healthy,* like an *animal. Good liver, good lung!*" Even Frabbie, when she had borne the babies, her conscience as clear as a fish's as she lay back on the sheets; her head turned, with the dead child in the room, toward some truth as cool and smooth as a river stone or sturgeon's egg.

Perhaps it all comes down to that first breath, how quickly it is grabbed, he thinks.

How each of his five children fought against that savage, swift indrawing—they had to be swung by the doctor by their heels around the room, lips puckered in a wince, as though, even if they took that breath at last and made their first frail mew, they had to think about it, as if they could not fathom other people's instincts.

In his son Freddie, undistinguished in the army, there is still that fine hesitation, an invisible vowel, before he speaks. He suspects that little pause has cost him.

He thinks again of how to put himself on paper.

His envy, watching De Rudio with the trumpet listen briefly for a melody, feel some fresh intelligence within his breath, and then bear down upon it.

It was he who insisted on this ghost garden. Seeds he mailed Frabbie during his service, pressed into the pages of his letters, asking her to plant them. He stands here now, behind the house, to watch the squirrels throw their weight among the bushes at the edges of the shadow.

In the early days they had also posted pubic hair to one another on the steamers. She would write, *I have found some more of that* wild thyme *you are so fond of.*

The first ghost garden that he saw was in the back yard of a cheap hotel outside New Orleans; its front bar the usual slow aquarium of grievance. The manager, a woman, had read about the this new fad in some smart book, and made her own little silver garden out of pots. If she found one of the men had stabbed his cigarette out on a hairy leaf she ran into the bar and screeched. The men would laugh and throw their hatbands at her, then turn back to their talk.

The squirrels grasp the tree trunks with their hefty forearms. They move so fast that a camera could not catch them, head and tail suddenly reversed, greedy hearts suspended.

Afterward, he would enumerate the dead for Freddie out here.

This one for McInnes, who said, I am at the bottom of the sea, before he put the gun inside his mouth and pulled the trigger.

Buford, also from the South, who hunted by the alphabet, who boasted that he had eaten everything from *A* to *P*; who, when he met a woman, let her feel the little pelts he carried in his pockets.

Jones, who played imaginary drums upon his collarbones . . .

Some days he walks out here and swears he hears their conversation. The squirrels move like children cheating at a game, one craven eye on whether he is watching. Finding Freddie, one day, when he was little, pouring tea upon the silver leaves to warm them.

The squirrels' tails are feathery, shot through with reddish light; the hair is sparse, the curved flesh greyish underneath. They remind him of a woman's pubic brush.

What is it the boy wrote? *My belief in the fundamental goodness of a man much put-upon . . .*

Yet he wonders if he has not always been dark-hearted.

One time, years before the battle, when Freddie was ten months old and sitting in the garden in his high-chair, he had said to Frabbie, "He is good in spite of being a baby"—a kind of pleasant reflex, brought on by the sunlight, he did not pause to think the words through. We are all born sinners, he had added.

Frabbie did not speak to him for days—the one time she had slapped him.

Another bar in Texas, from those days of drinking. There was a man whose friends would use him as a table every time he passed out. They would tell him, when he woke beneath their forks and plates, that he was in the hospital, that the doctor had just sawn his leg off. And he would sink back, steeped in his own pain, with the stony inward pleasure of a saint.

He stands among the cold leaves for a long time with the letter in his hand.

Handsome Jack, at Fort Riley, who had started up the Grand Order of the Grapefruit.

He invented silly names for each of them, secret greetings they exchanged across the sagebrush. He drew a blank-eyed face upon the fruit that he had found on a trader's boat one morning. As the weeks passed it would turn up, its expression blanker and more shrivelled, on a window ledge or hanging from the branches of a plum tree.

His insistence that they cape themselves and slake their thirst each week upon the altar of the little wizened god.

Star-Gazer, peering like a frog over the wet edge of his glass, confiding that he had once had his watch stolen from him by a gang of children in a city, who had baled him up behind a flower seller's cart.

Himself, shaken pissless into waves of silent laughter at the sight of Pritzker, passed out, rouge on his cheeks that they had put there, a handkerchief still tied up in a bow beneath his chin.

De Rudio, with that big grin, raising up his glass and saying "*Sup*-er!"

Handsome Jack again, lifting his chin to heaven as he sang with Jones's banjo his ditties in praise of the shy nocturnal thoughts of grapefruit.

And afterward, leering at them all across his drink, filled with that faith in brotherhoods that drove him—as if they too were ripe, vine-ready fruits that he had plucked.

Sometimes he wondered about that act Star-Gazer and Handsome Jack had going—if they did not disappear into the bullberries late at night to speak some other, sober language.

They seemed to have always been here in the army, as if they had sprung full-formed from air.

One morning, stiff with nightbruise, Benteen had woken early and lay still on his bedroll. A quarter-moon still clung to the sky's edge; he could smell thin smoke from the cook's tent; a mouse moved back and forward in the high grass behind his head as if it could not yet believe in their existence. That quiet feel of sleep which stretched across the ground like mist before the men woke up.

He heard their voices rising softly from the little gulch behind him.

He could not see them, but he felt how they were sitting. Handsome Jack, with his arms behind his head, his feet halfway up the dry wall. Star-Gazer in his usual squat, one hand on his chin.

Handsome Jack was telling of how he had eaten a bad oyster after the theater late one evening. How, in his cravat and waistcoat, he had had to drop his trousers in a back lane, his balls chiming in the breeze, the pale globe of his ass-flesh shining like a second moon beneath the gas light.

Once, Star-Gazer replied, after three days at the fair, he had developed sores at the corners of his mouth from eating cotton candy and had had to see a doctor.

They stopped talking for a moment.

Benteen heard Handsome Jack balance and bounce a pebble on his shoe, then kick it at some insect.

It was his life's ambition to achieve the amiable fuck, Handsome Jack said, and gave that off-hand laugh as light as chaff.

Benteen imagined Star-Gazer toying with his buttons, his hair hanging down across his eyes, then squinting at the sunrise.

I'm looking for an excuse myself, Star-Gazer said at last.

The others dead:

Sumner who said once that no one in all his life had ever posted him a letter.

Madden who ate grass when he was nervous.

There are no ducks now, upon the water, in the heat.

He thinks again of the night before the battle. When the woman had taken the coins they passed to Young Tom, she strode ahead, her feet swift in the heavy boots, as if she did not notice that they breathed so close behind her. She lay down in the river then, as she had promised. The chill water in the soft hollows of her body, she tilted back her long throat, as if to balance a second, secret moon upon her breastbone. An image he had then as he stood there, of some animal that would come down later from those pale mountainsides to drink, picking its careful way between the sods that they had churned up. Their hearts quickening. The urge to touch the white dress that she had folded, so light it did not seem to touch the mud.

Sometimes, as he sits there on the landing with his shoes off, he expects to see her, suspended just beneath the river's muddy surface, her face impassive, staring upward like a pike.

Something else Star-Gazer wrote:

It may be, in the future, that you will require no particular understanding of the past, but only of the present. For it is your time that makes us. It is you Custer thinks of and you he knows. As cunning and self-centered as a mollusk which

knows nothing but the tide it waits for, but this it under-
stands entirely . . .

Custer's legend still growing even now, their corpses tied
to his, their reputations measured by his actions.

A crawfish he had seen once in a market in New Orleans,
the blue slick upon its back, its feelers touching at the air
before it, the last alive upon a silver pile of others dead.

How to explain it to the boy.

It took place afterward. Their existence not in the confu-
sion of the battle but in those facts that settled later, the
words that floated to the surface. Those who lived surprised
to see what other selves turned up in the courtroom and in
books. As for the dead, it is the internals that perish first, he
thinks, in history as in death, the brute shape of the bone that
carries on.

For himself, he wants to say, all he remembers some days
is standing on the prairie in his boots; the pleasure of their
shape around his calves, the sense of himself after all that
riding as a mammal walking upright.

History another battle.

A dash into the big nothing, the mystery of air behind
them.

On the riverbank he sees five turtles, eyes eternal and unblinking, lined up along a muddy tree root. A sharp urge to follow his young self as he dives into this same water, the hot sun carried in upon his shoulders, his sturdy heart enjoying its brief stillness—to follow his own slick mammal stream back up to the surface, tight bubbles clinging to the hair upon his thighs.

When he received that last note that Custer sent—*Bring Pacs*—his first thought, even as he caught a glimpse of Reno's troops, was that the bastard couldn't even spell it.

At the trial afterward, they had all remarked upon his own calmness, urged his promotion to Major Benteen; made it clear how, in spite of Custer's note to join him, time and land had closed between him and the hope of getting packs and bullets to the rest.

He watches as his shadow turns before him, skims along the bank. The turtles, as one, drop into the water.

He thinks, how small the river is.

It has never been much more than a path to the grist-mill, no great and mythic passage here; some premonition his father must have had about the Benteen name.

For a while he thinks of nothing but such bitter symbols for his life.

Rogers, who, whenever he insulted you, always added, And one for the horse you came on.

Simkin's stories of stupid sign posts he had seen.

Willis, who, when referring to Rogers always sighed and said, Too much circus, too little brain.

Marsh, haunted to eterenity by the hobo who had come up to him once in New York City and said, When I was young like you are now, my life ran like water.

INSIDE THE ICE HOUSE AGAIN his heart beats slowly like a reptile's. Muscle and haunch frozen in the pit beneath him. Old pollens rising up from ticking ice cracks. A sense, in this grainy vapor, of some blank mind taking in his shape, the staleness of his crotch.

The first time he and Frabbie did it.

A willingness and looseness about her that he had not suspected, nor the heat inside her. The shock as her finger entered there. He was surprised to hear himself yell out.

Afterwards, a great bowel anxiety, a night of acid tumble-turns inside his stomach. He had to go out walking in the morning. The feeling that he needed to apologize—but more than this, his sense of pity for them both. A terrible sameness about all of us.

A name he thought of it by. The World of Sex.

For the next two months he snuck around the house as if it was a city. He lurked behind the settee, read the spines of books. The parlor was main street. He had his town face on, as if he might be seen by gossips. His wife a stranger he did not want to meet.

She did not press or ask him questions. She was also quiet, often reading from a book of poems. He loitered in the study, did not come to bed.

Something she said, years later, about his anger then, his shoes laced tight, his silence in the teacups. He remembers it as the silken flare of fear.

At last her father invited him to visit, the quart between them as they sat out on the veranda; he glanced without interest over the documents Benteen had brought for him to look at. A hard man with a squint, two thin lines between his eyes, dark eyebrows pluming. As Benteen left, he slipped him the envelope, said he might make use of these special picture cards from France.

The same sense he had of public shame, years later, when the doctor drew his foreskin back with his cool fingers and slid the tip of the catheter in. Walking through the main street, the sense of hard silver still filling the inside spaces of his cock.

It was not until years later, as the cult of Custer grew, that he realized how little he had understood then; he felt his life grow insubstantial, that same high-pitched buzzing in his ears as he had heard upon the ridge. But back then, as he'd stood unharmed among the Indians' bullets and urged the men on, he had been sustained by some great idea of fairness, the firm knowledge that our actions make us, a near-religious faith in sweat and lead.

Strange how, when the bullet grazed his thumb, he had thought, as if it belonged to someone else, *that finger there is injured* and continued on.

But Whittaker. That biography of Custer, whispered in his ear by the widow, who would have you believe that she had mated with a saint. No word of how Custer, against Benteen's advice, had split the Seventh into three and dashed off chasing glory; how Benteen, further down the valley with his men, had found Reno's troops in disarray, led them with his own men toward that ridge, and saved their lives. Not enough for the public, though. He used to say, when he was liquored up, *They hunger for their gods most who do not stand and fight.*

There were whole days in the years that followed when the lies churned inside his head; others when he could think of nothing but the idea of corresponding, although he did not know with whom.

That rare sense, on the ridge, of accommodation to the air around him that he feels only the faintest inkling of now as he peels an egg or shreds his pipe plug on the step.

A terrible thing, suddenly, to haunt yourself, to pile up

evidence of what you were, to explain yourself to strangers. Some strange urge, too, to cast aside the good opinions he had earned, as not worth having. He would say to Frabbie, *We are not what we have done but what people think they know about us.* His life now an imitation of itself—something apart but attached, like that injured thumb. Some days he is outraged for his name—others so sick of it he wishes he could call the surgeon in to cut it off.

Sometimes, Frabbie said last night, when the maid had left the room, it was not sex but surfaces she craved.

When he was away upon the plains she had stood in the street and imagined a pair of hands pressed against her waist, it did not matter whose. No particular tone to what she said. Her neck, as she spoke, was still and supple, all at once—it seems to him that she has been the same age always.

When he was away, she said, she dreamed of flat cotton sheets, of kid gloves, of silver oyster forks, of drawers with polished china handles.

Pritzker, dreaming for three nights running that he had a banana on a leash, which, he said, was quite affectionate.

Grasshopper Joe telling the story one afternoon of how he had ridden into a strange canyon filled with pyrites, and lost his memory for two days after.

De Rudio, one night, when Benteen found him playing his trumpet softly in the mess, telling him solemnly, I am suffering from *Bier Angst*.

Handsome Jack's list of ways to announce, from the bushes, that he had just relieved himself:

Thar she blows; Bingo!; The chocolate shop is open; Ooh la la; Those pups need feeding; Bellhop!; Anyone for marbles?; I have been insulted; This cake needs frosting; It is a sorry child that does not know his father; Enough wax to seal a letter; Polish it up and put it in your reticule; The night watch has been relieved; Heeere's Fred!

Nyow! Handsome Jack appears beside him at the bar.

His back teeth are well afloat, the glass of bug-juice cradled daintily; a surly tenderness about the way he holds it.

Evening virgins, he says to Sully and his mates, seated in the corner.

Star-Gazer squeezes in at Benteen's other side, his cuffs drooping in the pooled-up liquid on the bar. His black hair is flattened in the heat into two limp bangs above his glasses. He leans up and shouts in Benteen's ear, Handsome Jack just asked me if I had ever had a snifter with a poofter. His eyes behind each greasy lens are wide with mocked-up shock.

Nyow! Handsome Jack says again, nods with gravitas, then flashes Benteen a beardy leer.

His eyes, in spite of drunkenness, are covertly attentive. A sense that he has some rule book for hard drinking that the others lack. There is still the chance that if he does not sense the presence of that higher power that will take him almost to his self's edge, some invented passion or game of cards beyond his league, he will stay like this all night, refuse all conversation.

At the sound of a banjo from the far end of the room Handsome Jack does a little shimmy, hips pushed forward, meaty rear tucked in; a coquette's shy delight in his copious endowment as it moves in little arcs from side to side.

Hey Scruggs, he calls out across the room, Have you ever mustered in Custer's cluster?

Scruggs and the others scowl and tighten in a smaller knot around the table. Burton the Whale picks at his thick white palm; Ambrose the Bilk mutters something low to Sully, who laughs high-pitched and spits.

And now it seems Handsome Jack is alive on bar air. His grey skin is asheen and almost pink.

It is like this. He is trying the evening on for all of them, making sure it fits. There is a force, he knows, within the night, intended just for them, some great defining moment.

Our perfect selves, or the abyss—Star-Gazer, in his notes, on Handsome Jack.

A bar in Kansas with an old pear tree by the gate that the men had used so often as a john, they said, the fruit was filled with piss.

Who knows, he thinks that he will write now to the boy, *but that all our history may exist at the mercy of our scribes, that even now a hundred Greek and Roman and Egyptian Whittakers, bowing and scraping before their mediocre heroes and desiring to take some reflected glory on themselves, do not yet lead us by the hand.*

In Montana they cut through the surface of the river to let the horses drink. Weird green clouds pressed down on the mountains; the pines a royal blue, like the ruched insides of glaciers, in the clearer air beneath. The only way to find the sullen ice-streams sometimes was to sight the yellowed marsh grass at their edges.

Handsome Jack, lost to them for some time now, stood apart and smoked a cigarette which someone in the Choir had offered, staring out across the snowy plain. Star-Gazer, too, had withdrawn himself, hunched on the pebbles and fiddling with his horse's hoof, his breath a grainy haze. He had begun already to compose in his head the pages that he would ball up and throw into the campfire every evening.

No sign yet of the Indians although Custer seemed more jumpy now, as if he traced some secret scent in that unruffled coldness.

A dark patch of soil beside Benteen where a bison had hunkered on its forelegs while the snow came.

He thought—a silence without conscience, no hint of supple thought within it.

Not just him. He watched De Rudio, his coarse red face duller with the cold, his smile gone, frowning as he stamped from foot to foot and eyed the mountains.

Handsome Jack, caught watching Custer as he and Young Tom sighted with their rifles through the blankness, gave Benteen a nasty little smile and nodded.

Star-Gazer cupped his hands and drank the water.

The thin malevolence of eras, he would write later in his journal, *cold untroubled centuries of fish and stone.*

Someone in the Choir let out a long, low whistle as Benteen turned back toward his horse. The clouds came down among them as it began to snow again. And in that one moment he knew himself as he would always be, dry-eyed and unrequited.

Unthinkable to him now, his limbs' slick weightlessness when he was the same age as the boy. A memory, suddenly, of how he used to see strange cities in his mind's eye, walking; shadowed avenues and distant clocks and birds he did not recognize that flocked around their fountains; some hint even of the mysterious quilted air of other continents that pricked within his muscles as he strode.

That was youth, he thinks—so relentless in its drive to stretch its empires outward.

In Dakota Handsome Jack swore that he was shitting landscapes.

Red clay, grey shale, the dark blue anticline of cliff face, he said it all had some effect the other way, in the twists and turns and colors that he squeezed out. He evolved a theory that it came from all the riding, the texture passed up through the horse's feet, translated through the ass-gut and repeated, like the music roll within a pianola.

Looks familiar, he would say, passing by two shrivelled, knobby bits of granite in the grass.

Why did he like Handsome Jack, Benteen wonders, when he despised Custer for his crudeness? Because he always bedded down his horse before he ate, because his games were games, not practice. His drinking charter: they had to get the word *corn* into every sentence that they spoke or take another swig. The little sketches that he did of Pritzker's cat dreams.

And then there were the miseries that also struck him sometimes when he drank, when he would grow a beard he did not shave for weeks, when he would speak into the night of the indignities of God and sex. God has no memory, he would say.

He remembers Handsome Jack's howls of delight when Star-Gazer told them how he had gone to the theater one night and found, perched on the toilet seat, a perfect dinosaur that someone had constructed out of turds and matchsticks.

Custer then.

He cannot be avoided.

In Kansas, in his first years with the Seventh, he took the best ambulance for his hounds. His wife had another fitted as a carriage, calling for him from within with some little chore or to ask him who he thought she ought to write to. The sick men on their horses with what they called dry twitches from the heat, forced to ride ahead as Custer disappeared into its tender shade for hours.

The dogs had the same rations as the men, a thought that turned them off their bacon. The quick way the beasts inhaled it, the way they seemed to turn it in a second into muscle. He had found one of their teeth once, bloodless as a shark's, in the dirt beside the campfire where they ate.

One day the ambulance hit a bump and the doors which someone had left deliberately unlatched flew open. A pair of dogs in full rut landed on the road—two males, they quickly noticed—and did not stop as Custer flew in with a whip, amid the roars and howls and whistles of the men. The top dog seemed pleased with the attention; he kept on at it, a look of glassy concentration on his face beneath the lashing of the quirt, as if he pushed a buggy in a sideshow.

They gave Custer a hard time after that. Your dog sent them, they would say, when he found the posy on his saddle. He wishes to know if you are free this evening. General, I have a bone your dog might like.

They hated the dogs but they did not hate him.

This he must also make clear—men fear above all to hate each other. We are the true coquettes, he thinks, prepared to forgive each other almost anything in order not to have to fight.

$$\asymp$$

Ice sullen in the pit beneath him.

Evans, when he delivers it, says that you can see the silent pond-depths in the blocks when they are brought down off the train, ranged from eerie green to palest brown. He slowly smokes his cigarette, and lays his hands along their sides as if they are the flanks of cattle.

He waits patiently while Benteen stoops and pokes beneath the tarpaulin on the truck bed; he never takes ice himself, he says, but prefers a cup of something hot.

A shop in New Orleans that he saw once, a single block of ice laid out in the window on a cloth, a crowd stopped to view the sturgeon caught inside it.

In England, Evans says, they get their ice from Norway; the men standing with their iron saws upon the fiords, the blocks put on a wooden slipway, where they glide quietly past fir and reindeer to the ships.

There is a particular blue, he says, from way down in the deepest lakes, that does not wish you good, that troubles with your mind.

His family had got their money from printing up sheet music: *Bouquet de Mélodies, Potpourri Pour Le Piano.*

It became his way with Frabbie to sing them. And to Freddie later when he cried.

If she was upset—*Away with Melancholly.* Or, tremolo, *Night-Daws are Weeping,* amorous and cat-like. Until she had to put down the book or hairbrush that she held and laugh. If he came across her kneeling looking for a button— *I'm Dreaming, Oh I'm Dreaming.* His cool, shaved cheek against hers, he did not say, I love you. Instead, *Come to the Sunset Tree, Oh Share My Cottage.*

Sometimes, at the table, impatient for them to be left alone, he had hummed the *Gold-Fever Gallop,* softly, with his eyebrows raised, to let her know he wished to go to bed.

They hated her, though—Libbie Custer.

That crimped ambitious mouth, those little teeth. Her eyes filled with a dark hunger, so that she later learned to twist her head in photographs to hide it.

She turned each sentence with an irony so precisely obscu-rative that she made it a kind of game to find her out within it. Is that a fact? Do you think so, now? Her face a mask of comic wisdom until you wondered if anyone ever had a true opinion on this earth. Her voice mock-Irish as she held her husband's gaze and flirted: It is a nice day indeed, General. Thanks be to the One Above, she added.

They had a dim inkling even then that she was playing games not just with them but with the future; that she saw them as corpses already, to be humored.

They had instructions from Custer to kill her if it looked like a defeat, and some mornings they would sit and draw lots to determine who would have the privilege if this turned out to be the day. Yet if she emerged from the prim shade of her quarters, looking for some leaf to decorate her cook's pie or a colored stone to post off to her nephews, they fell over to fulfill her little wishes.

Walking through the camp, scissors in her hand to trim the General's hair, humming to herself, she watched to see if they were watching. He believed she had no private thoughts, only, like Custer, a kind of extra instinct for standing where the light would catch her best.

A modern talent, this, to live on the outside of your skin. Another piece of wisdom for the boy.

Outside, he looks at the photograph again.

This time, in the damp glare, he notices the pin-stripes on the boy's pants; long shiny knees that suggest enormous feet below the edges of the frame. The suit is tight around the armpits and he senses the bulk of more than one wet handkerchief wadded in internal pockets; library tickets, too, no doubt, and notes scribbled in a fever of ideas upon a crowded trolley bus while others stand.

A parlor painted on the backdrop, in which the photographer has forgotten to unruche a chalky pleat.

The boy has tightened some mental sphincter in response to the exposure: his face is *adjusted*.

He remembers, suddenly, how, during their leave from the academy, he had come across Freddie and his friends in their new uniforms beneath the mulberry, caught up in some long-running argument over whether rocks were alive; Ah yes, but can you *prove* they have no feelings, he heard one of them drawl; they lay back on their elbows with their pipes lit and looked up at him, when he appeared, with faces utterly composed, as amoral and implacable as kittens'; his strange shame as if he had trodden in something soft there in their mossy parlor.

He fantasizes for a moment that he has a goat, so that he can feed it the boy's photograph in tiny pieces.

Can this be history, is that all it comes down to, as Custer may have guessed, this scrutiny of a face and its relationship to light?

There are things, he thinks, that he ought not to leave out.

The way the men called the shells they used "little pups,"and kissed or smacked them on their cold behinds before they loaded them.

How, when they wrote letters, they would make a point of folding them so tight that they would fit like a secret in a woman's palm.

The time the river flooded at Fort Larned and they woke to a stinking bank covered with knives and forks and spoons, dug in upright on their ends.

Monroe said that cows would follow you, as if they wanted to ask you a question; it could drive you crazy sometimes to try to work out what it was.

That old Irish line of Keogh's that he guaranteed with women—he would brush their fingertips with his and say, If you wish, I guarantee, it will rain tonight. They would pause for a moment, at last deciding on the poetry, and open up their doors.

The slow sheen of the river, now, passing and repassing. The boy's letter stiff within the pocket of his suit breast, the hot sun on his eyelids.

Something else Star-Gazer said, he cannot quite remember—about history being the sum of the griefs we choose, more than the triumphs . . .

There was one time, long before the battle and between campaigns, when he came down here to visit. Sliding about on the flat footpaths in his new shoes. Swearing that he had woken on the steam train late at night, looked straight into another window, and seen the butcher blow his nose on a piece of liver, put it back. Saying, as he slipped across the spongy town squares and clasped his dark hat to his head, I feel like a parrot on an ice rink.

The only time Star-Gazer and his wife would meet since she stayed here in Georgia with their boy.

Afterward he and Frabbie would remark that during those two days they could not remember one single detail Star-Gazer had told them of himself, or anything that they had done together. Just that one glimpse they had had of him in the park down near the docks, sitting cross-legged on a bench, his back to the balconies and high warm walls and idling carriages, as if the town was a closed book that he knew by heart already; an unchewed apple on the seat beside him; his eyes closed as though he took some grim dictation from the sun which had burned through the sea mist that in the mornings drifted up the river. A dim memory of Frabbie's from her schooling, of those northern races who sat on the ice floes with their faces to the east to await whatever incarnation followed on from death.

Frabbie told Star-Gazer as he left, Until we met I had not believed that you existed.

His thin valise was empty except for the lunch that she had had the maid pack.

Star-Gazer replied that he himself was not so certain of it yet.

There were fish in some of the Texan rivers, Monroe said, named lickerfish; you would squat in the water to drop your wax and feel very wanted.

Melville kept an old sock hanging off his banjo's tuning pegs.

Reynolds always liked to shout when he was drunk, The shrimp is a mystery to man!

It was Handsome Jack who hated her the most; long before Rat Friday when he had his Revelation.

This powdery Kansas morning Custer had them riding cover, watching out for Indians: Monroe the cowboy, Scruggs, and Bender; Benteen, Star-Gazer, and Handsome Jack. Libbie and some of the officers' wives had begged Custer and Young Tom to take them shooting. They had sat up all night at their sewing: brocade at their breasts, epaulets upon their sleeves, yellow sashes round their waists. As they passed out through the fort's gates they saluted brightly, gentle De Rudio persuaded to play *Garry Owen* as they rode.

The men lagged behind on the edges of the sycamores, until soon they could only see Young Tom cutting behind the women with the hounds.

Let the Indians have her, said Monroe.

Poor devils, Bender answered.

Did they remember, Star-Gazer asked, the time the cook had made the poison pies that made the entire camp sick? All but her, he said, she had loved hers. He had seen her eat the whole thing up.

That was because she was the most venomous thing you might meet with on a prairie, said Benteen, she was immune.

The cook put a dead horse in the filling once, Star-Gazer continued. An awful thing, to find an eye in your pie, as he had done.

She could out-fang anything, said Scruggs.

All this while Handsome Jack had ridden silent, his dignity

wrapped tight around him. With that special tenderness he had for insult, he was afflicted by her very presence; not by what she said, but what she seemed to make of them behind her smile. She would say *Good day, Captain*, each syllable pronounced, her blue eyes fixed on yours, he had said before, as if she fathomed all your secrets.

Handsome Jack shrugged. It's the neurotic ones who are the best in bed. They're so eager to please they'll do anything you ask.

Far ahead, Young Tom leaned out in his saddle to catch in his mouth the peanuts Libbie threw. And Handsome Jack, for the first time that day, seemed to rouse himself, as a mysterious little triumph flashed across his face. The closest he came to a religion, sometimes, to predict the worst and see it carried out.

The fundamental question, he said, grinning now, is this— is she a grunter or a groaner? A screamer or a squeaker?

He urged his horse into a canter. His shadow skipped and skimmed in the weak dazzle of the morning. And you can bet she makes that fucker pay the price, too, he called back, makes him go the vinegar lick. Hey Custer! he shouted, gaining on the party. You quim-quaffer! You gusset-guzzling bloomer-bolter! You old tuft-taster!

Star-Gazer, for once, did not ride along beside him, but stopped and fiddled with his glasses in the shade.

Young Tom, not quite in earshot, turned to meet them, a thin suspicion on his features.

Handsome Jack offered up a sweet smile, but in such a

way there could be no doubt there had been some disturbing forethought in its composition.

Wild turkey, he told Custer when he rode up—Over in the bushes. He pointed back to where the men stood.

Handsome Jack tipped his hat to Libbie and the ladies, winked.

They might make a nice pie, he said.

⌖

That's a strange title for a book, isn't it? Star-Gazer asked one day. What do you mean? said Young Tom. Star-Gazer smoothed his hair from crown to cheeks. You don't think so? The General must have his reasons, I suppose. At last Young Tom cracked and told him to spit out what he meant. Star-Gazer looked embarrassed and played with the buttons on his shirt. Well, he said, it just seems . . . don't you think? . . . unusual—*My Lie on the Plains.*

For the next week, if any of them spoke to him, he swore that he'd gone deaf.

⌖

Throughout that whole picnic lunch, Star-Gazer and Handsome Jack sat on either side of Libbie Custer like two knowing saints, their mouths straight lines, their eyelids dry and heavy. Let me pass you the salt, Handsome Jack said. No ma'am, the honor is all mine. Vinegar? Star-Gazer asked.

Here, at the river, he lets the morning take him. It is so quiet that he can almost hear the crisp wings of the dragonflies on the other side as they dip above a boat lying half-sunk in the rushes.

He thinks he might bring the paper down here to the landing, but it is Frabbie these days who unfolds it in the parlor—she needs no spectacles—and reads it through intently as if it might still provide answers to the human puzzle. She sometimes takes the scissors from the kitchen and neatly clips an article to send to Freddie and his wife. She has not come, as he does, to only see one single story in it.

In the evenings the shrimp flip as slick and light as fingernails across the water, chased by the bigger fish below. Sometimes they dig themselves into the mud, long feelers afloat, their veined backs showing; once you have pulled them from the water they resign themselves instantly to death, lying damp and listless in your hand.

He must tell the boy, he thinks, how it was to meet the Indians in battle.

At the Washita, eight years before Bighorn, their orders to take Black Kettle's camp by stealth.

Fear his geography, as much as the low diversion of the hills, or the flies around his horse's head, he rides down astride it. Too late if he thinks to weave or flinch; instead, he puts his mind a half-second ahead into that holy pocket of the air where he knows the arrows will not find him. Flashes of uncolored thought—*Sully's mount is lame, that squaw has caught an arrow in the spinal.* No, not true that he has never had a quiet moment in his life; he knows himself now only as a white man fighting, the gun as familiar in his hand as the hot shape of his horse's eye beneath the lid when he sponges it at night. With a stranger's curiosity, he imagines himself with his entrails opened out across a rock, his mouth agape, far gone beyond the nudity of sex. The Cheyennes shrieking. He does not hate them, the same language of haunch and hot intestine underneath them; it is different with the women, but with the men he feels it is all fate.

Afterward, a hard blood echo in the frozen ground; some warm animal reflux hanging on for hours within the churned-up air.

Custer takes the old chief's scalp, the sound like a runner pulled up from the lawn.

Some agitation among Sully and the Choir over near the willows; the pulpy hoots and cries of schoolboys; something moving there . . .

A beaded dress abandoned in the tents along with the dried meat and the furs, a young woman's shape held perfectly within the softness of the deerskin; he remembers Star-Gazer squatting down beside it for a long time with his cigarette unlit.

Hard days for Frabbie in those last dark years of his service, when she came up to Fort DuChesne to join him. He would blow a cloud if anyone brought whiskey near their quarters. If she asked him what he would like to eat, or whether he would care to go out for a walk, he would only look at her and say, *I do not know.*

An image of himself, suddenly, in the days before they granted him the discharge, relieving himself on the outside of a tent while the ladies were inside; turning to repeat to the young officer who gently guided him through the streets Pritzker's phrase, *I am as happy as a saucer.*

After the Washita, they had to kill the Indians' ponies. Eight hundred of them, herded with the donkeys in a circle, watchful and still, nostrils flaring, as if united by a single twitching nerve.

Glancing at De Rudio, who says, softly, *Ja. Do it*. Then beginning with the knife.

He thinks of the boy now, in Chicago, standing in the kitchen with his careful meal of toast and cheese, peering out the window; or on a park bench, his knees pressed together, champing dreamily upon a currant bun that he has bought from a girl he fancies in a shop.

He sees the boarding house, with its grimy sign, the clippings stacked carefully beside the boy's bed, the kittens feeding from their mother on a low shelf of the cupboard.

This is his lone disciple.

Lips pressed into a thin smile, he heads toward the study and takes out a piece of paper.

Sir, how are the cats? he writes.

Handsome Jack's hobbies.

At Fort Dodge there is a manual that Handsome Jack studies. He claims to have waved a gold watch before Star-Gazer's eyes and made him walk across the fire coals with his boots off; Star-Gazer plays along with it, asks out of the blue as they are riding if they have seen his socks, if anyone else is haunted by the smell of bacon.

At Fort Hays, the two of them have a bet to see who can fit the most clichés into a conversation without Custer or his brother guessing. One hot afternoon they come across Young Tom by the horse trough, wetting his kerchief before he ties it back around his neck. He tells them Custer has sprained his ankle on the way to the latrines and has to spend the next few days inside his cabin. A damned shame, says Handsome Jack. That's too bad, Star-Gazer agrees and pulls his hat down further, you've got to keep your wits about you in the dark. Young Tom says that he is to take Libbie for her morning rides now. Handsome Jack appraises him a moment longer than he needs to.

Yairs, he says, I guess it's either one little thing or the other.

He catches Star-Gazer's eye, a dirty tremor at the corner of his mouth, and the two men melt in fits of silent laughter.

In his desk he finds one of those old pictures of the Seventh. He will show it to the boy—this is how it feels to live within a country that has not yet been invented.

You can see it in the blurred meanness of Simms' face, the wolf-like suspicion in the whites of Sully's eyes, the blaze of Burton's beard in all directions, Monroe the cowboy's bug-eyed camera stare. In the last months they have ridden always on the edge of cloud shadow; they have picked their way up a mountain by the moon's light only; they have seen a young Sioux throw his arms around his horse's neck and say to it, I love you, as he died. When the scout translated later, he had felt a sensation familiar and unfamiliar all at once.

If you look carefully, he thinks, you will see how we carried the idea of the Indians within us always.

The thought of a gun always darkening our footsteps, the plains eternal grey behind us.

You can see it there in the face of Grasshopper Joe—a certain knowledge that what we have witnessed here cannot be surpassed.

Star-Gazer's notebook: *I do not think the soul is a good thing if given infinite space.*

He could send Keogh into a blazing rage by telling the others that *Garry Owen* was not Irish; it had been invented by a salesman in Pittsburgh.

We Benteens have been in the sheet music business for generations, he would say, so I think we ought to know.

The men's pets—

Massie had a goose that nibbled on his eyebrows, Dufault two owls because he liked the way they ate, Monroe the cowboy a porcupine called Gorgeous.

For a brief time, in Dakota, there was a blacktail deer with a slimy nose that suckled from the pack mare.

Pritzker's pelican rode before him on the pommel like a stern god.

Sully's cougar cub. He would blow smoke up his sleeve

while he held it in his jacket. When released, it roared and staggered like a drunk.

Grasshopper Joe had turned a wooden box into a mansion for his insects. He held up his *girls*, as he called them, and admired their little waists, the long lean muscles of their thighs. He put cigarette-paper sheets upon their beds. He fed them moth wings from his lips. When bored he whittled tiny birchwood chairs and tables.

Amazing the creatures they had collected on that last campaign. Each man with an animal like some ghostly thought that would not abandon him.

Mice, salamanders, prairie chickens. Jack rabbits, a white fox, three antelopes, an eagle. Rogers' blind quail that nodded in his kerchief.

Their sense, at night, of those small chests pulsing in the darkness as they slept; a soft moonlit telegraph of watchful hearts.

When was it, Fort Lincoln, after all the years of forts and tenting, when he began to notice the edge of an exquisite boredom at work in Handsome Jack?

He was discovering new passions almost daily: teaching

the Chinese cook's young son to curse, composing fake sermons around some silly subject that the men had chosen, collecting verse, then songs, about big noses. One snowy afternoon he took a chair outside the fort and sat with his back against the wall, little bits of biscuit in his fingers, training Custer's dogs to come to Libbie's name.

One night when they were drunk together Handsome Jack told Benteen that he had seen the ghost of his dead father standing by his bunk.

He drank harder by this time, lying on his bunk, giggling at some private joke; juggling lead shot, and leaving the pieces on the blanket where they fell.

Once he beckoned Benteen to come and see a huge castle he had built out of cards on the long table in the mess room; he stood there silently as Benteen praised it, gave a curt little bow and swept the turrets and towers off the table with his hand.

At the risk of blowing my own trouser trumpet, he said when Benteen found him, one midnight, playing draughts against himself, I don't need a lot of sleep.

⌖

When Libbie Custer said she had been invited by General Sherman's wife to take part in a *conversazione*, Star-Gazer hung forward on her words. He said, I tried Italian food once—doesn't it taste good?

This is what you did before a battle, he said to Frabbie last night; you had to fold your life like a jacket you would return to, and leave it with De Rudio and his trumpet, or in among the bushes; important to move weightless and unburdened toward your horse, otherwise your life's tender weight would trip you up.

And Frabbie asked him, Do you think this is a feeling women never have?

In the Black Hills, Star-Gazer claimed he had gone past writing into silence.

It seemed to him that whatever he crossed out from his notebook left its presence somehow on the page. The more he cut the more what he had left seemed filled with what had gone, its meaning hanging ghost-like in the spaces. Therefore, he said, with that strange, dogged squint, he had thought about it carefully, and decided that the most perfect book he wrote would be the one he did not write.

If he returned, Star-Gazer said—and Benteen is certain he said *if*, although he cannot imagine how he did not notice at the time—it was his ambition to find himself a group of writers whose qualification was that they did not write. They would recognize each other by sight and feeling, for it stood to reason they would never correspond. They would know themselves by a certain gravity of silence, by the works they refused and carried in their hearts.

He said this as they broiled the fish Benteen had caught.

With that frail incompetence he sometimes feigned, Star-Gazer was sitting with his arms clasped around his knees, staring at a long line of ants along the ground, while De Rudio smoked and tended to the fire. Benteen was working up a new rod from a length of birch. Monroe had turned the fishes' heads away toward the mountains, for he did not like the way they looked—too much underjaw and lip, he said.

They waited for Star-Gazer to continue, but he picked up a twig and examined it intently.

The half-moon blazed above them. A quarter-mile away the new railway track stopped among the stubble and prairie dog castles of the plains.

Into this silence Handsome Jack suddenly appeared, back from some secret mission in the woods, his beard awry, some belligerent edge now to the jaunty walk he put on to amuse them. He stabbed his fish with his pocket knife through the eye and dropped it on his plate.

Star-Gazer, he said, sometimes you're so funny I forget to laugh.

He is surprised to find himself upstairs in the bedroom, the waxed top of Frabbie's dresser cool as museum glass beneath his forearms. Calming, always, the soft integrity of wood, the patient memory of suppleness that seems to rest within it.

The counterpane is tight across the bed, the sun a relentless pressure on the shutters. The first thing he did when he returned from a campaign was to lean before the mirror like this in the half-light to calibrate the changes in his face; to breathe, like the air of some familiar, dustless planet, the lingering scent of his shoes in the armoire, the chill ivory backs of brushes, starch in handkerchiefs; smells of the unopened perfumes he has given Frabbie that have crept nonetheless into the letters and christening gowns she keeps in tissue in her dresser.

The knowledge that these things somehow reshaped him. Just as, on the long campaigns, he would smell the dust of his nails and whiskers in his razor and his clippers and know he was a soldier; taking comfort in the stale, hoofed odor of the male.

Why not start here? he thinks.

Tell the boy: it is not through the grand outlines of Custer's vision that we knew ourselves.

The individual rhythms of our horses' gaits, which we sometimes tried when bored to draw on paper; the shared vision of the last railway surveyor's peg far out beyond the Black Hills; the daily humilities of canvas and of leather—this is what we understood instead.

Custer again.

There is another memory of Custer, which strikes him now as urgent.

In Nebraska, patrolling near a narrow lake, they had come across a schoolroom in the woods. In its overgrown orchard, littered with apples too small and crabbed to eat, they saw a silent boy with leather splints tied to his shins, whose eyes were pale and filled with lake light. Girls, too, still as cranes in linsey dresses and unblinking. The whole place damp and cool, as if you had just turned back a lily pad. A tortoise, dark with soil from the hole that they had just dug, swallowed drily on the step.

A school for the deaf and dumb, the teacher said—she told the men they could put the fence back up if they were short of entertainment—and insisted Custer come inside. He strode in fast and stiff-hipped, as if to make his point.

Custer's puppy years back then, soon after he had married, when he was still unshaped around the edges. He scratched and showed his belly when he sat before a woman; he spoke rapid-fire; his punishments were harsh. Yet he possessed already, even then, an interesting kind of stillness, that seemed to settle on his shoulders like a gentle breeze from somewhere else, and take him by surprise.

Is this what the children saw—who touched, and retouched, the pockets of his coat?

When the teacher stamped her feet upon the floor, two of the older girls brought in a pot of tea, and milk. One of them tapped Custer on the shoulder and made a neat, quick gesture with her fingers. She would like to know if you want sugar, the teacher said, and Benteen could see the blond hairs on Custer's neck rise slightly at the touch. A couple of the younger girls, their smocked backs squashed up against the cupboard, were busy giggling with their hands.

It was the same sign language used by Indians, the teacher said.

Custer asked them how to make an egg, a heart, a vase, how to say the day is dawning; they took his delighted hands each time and forced them into signs.

Watery sunlight skipped and flickered in the room. For an hour, the children's hands portioned out the air. They plucked feelings from their chests with agile fingers; they took on the broad majesty of eagles, in pike and poise and dip; they made swift promises and tucked them in their hearts. It was a bright aquarium of fingers, it was a kingdom of the lakelit. Custer, serious and golden, looked as if he never wished to leave.

Afterwards, outside, Young Tom asked his brother what on earth he had been doing.

Custer grinned and turned his back and nodded to the teacher from his horse. Suddenly, he made Dandy rear up; he plucked an apple from a branch, threw it to the young boy, and before it had reached the top end of its flight, he wheeled away.

For the rest of the day, they would sneak these crabapples on his saddle if he stood for a moment in the stirrups. He brushed them off, his eyelids low, his shoulders languid.

He had found the shape of his own boastfulness.

And Benteen—sitting in his garden thinking of that apple's sweet and perfect arc through dappled light—even he cannot forget.

A dream he remembers suddenly, in which he is a shell tossed far out in the ocean in the center of a wave; a cool spiracle at his center through which the water rushes, filling and unfilling.

For some reason he thinks too of an afternoon long

before the children, when they were out walking, and Frabbie said, smiling, I dreamed last night before that I gave birth to a cat.

With that perfect sign language that would remain with him until his death, Custer pointed to his brother, drew feathers and a heavy breast and a little circle in the air.

Young Tom, smirking, smoothed his shirt and spread his loins.

What does that mean?

That you're a turkey's asshole, Custer said, and laughed until his face was wet.

STRANGE, HOW SOME THINGS SEEM to have an extra weight because of what is put inside them: photograph albums, mourning lockets, pocketbooks.

Opening his top drawer he finds his watch, with its miniatures of Frabbie and of Freddie as a child inside the lid; Frabbie has placed it here, in a cigar box, with his cufflinks and his pen, since he began to leave them in the kitchen with the flour, or among the duck shit and breadcrumbs on the landing.

And here, behind his medals, the ugly comb she wore in her hair for the first year of their marriage, that her mother gave her when she left—that he hid, finally, among the dried flowers in the fireplace—although later he kept it, and felt affection for it, because she had not seen the unkind intention in it. Or, he thinks suddenly, she did know, and wore it out of some firm, ascetic impulse.

This new knowledge takes him by surprise.

The Choir:

Scruggs kept a silver tumbler wound in a scarf inside his pack which was the only thing that he would drink from; each time they stopped he would unwind the cloth with a slow flourish, holding the cup against his belly, then grin and look around him.

Burton the Whale had a box of women's things that he took as "compensation" for the way that he'd been treated.

Maybliss had a dark mole on his lips that he picked at like a blister when depressed.

Marshall kept leeches on his arm beneath a bandage—his "restaurant"—letting them feed for days until they popped.

⤫

Star-Gazer wrote:

It is harder to commit to an idea than a country.

We are strung out along the periphery of a new thought, beyond the old shape of armies.

⤫

Pritzker said he would like to return to his old school and arm every student with a little whip.

Bender, when he made a good shot hunting, turned back toward them on his horse and made a dry little bow.

Monroe said his mother had the whitest eye that you had ever seen.

Interesting that the Indians also seemed to have this sense about a pocketbook; they might carry one about with them for years, emptied of its money, perhaps out of some feeling for the shallow curve it held from cleaving for so many years to an enemy's broad or sparrow chest.

Young Tom's birthday—christened "Rat Friday" by Handsome Jack. It was a date that had obsessed him for some weeks. He sat in the mess listening to them plan the outing, taking special exception to each item on their list, the buffalo salami or jugged hare; greeting each rug or cushion for the ladies that they itemized with a cheery *Woof, woof!*—he said the words, he did not bark—an affable smile upon his face, so that Young Tom and Custer did not quite know how to take it.

Back in their quarters he worked on a list of things that he would like to wish Young Tom upon this day: *fart fungus, toe-rot, scrotal scrofula.*

It would be too bad if he got a twisted tool, Star-Gazer said, his mouth slack and earnest.

And do not forget a punch in the cunt! De Rudio added.

Noted, my friend, Handsome Jack said, scribbling on the paper.

De Rudio nodded solidly, then bent to polish a smudge on a button with his sleeve. His shy pride made them laugh.

Later Handsome Jack would claim he had named the day because Custer had found a rat out on the trail the day before and put it in his pack for one of his dissections; that he had forgotten it and left it by the stables, where the horses were spooked all day by the stench of death, first like lamp gas, then like shit, at last combined into a solid earthy sweetness; and that he, Handsome Jack, had stood there grinning, struck by the thought that this smell was the landscape's grim, ironic language.

As the picnic party rode out—Young Tom spruiking in imitation of a fairground barker, Libbie tying a scarf around her husband's golden head as he came up to the trap and made the horse kneel before her—Handsome Jack had followed. He had watched as Custer urged the men on, Keogh, Young Tom, and Fitzwilliam. They approached the lake where a duck and her ducklings trod the water, the brood skittering like ballbearings back and forth across the surface to re-gather in her wake. Custer put up the challenge to see who could be the first to get their heads off.

Handsome Jack saw one small duck, lifted on a sudden geyser raised up by the bullets, treading the empty air with orange feet, and laughed. He heard Young Tom call out to Custer, You should know, you old show pony! while they raced on, and laughed again. Later he saw Libbie in the shade on the dark side of the lake with her hand inside the general's shirt, almost to the waist, as he leaned inside like a calf, eyes closed, and licked her neck—she met Handsome Jack's gaze, straight and cool, but kept on going—and at the sight he laughed and laughed and found he could not stop.

And so Handsome Jack got on his horse and rode further away from the direction of the fort, past crickets chittering in marsh grass, and the corpse of the buffalo onto which the officers had lifted their wives to make them scream; past the baize card tables and discarded women's shoes, out between the naked buttes; he was chuckling still, and whooping sometimes, as he pushed his horse into ravines where no grass grew, where he felt the shadows of birds pass as darker shadows on the cold faces of the cliffs, and heard the bellies of small lizards scrape against the rocks.

It was on the other, sunny, side of these great buttes that Handsome Jack had his Revelation.

These were the few details he told Star-Gazer when he came back that night, pallid and morose, a tremor in the corner of his eye:

There was a bright horizon in which the sun leaped and dazzled like a burning gate, and something soft and soulless just behind it; as it moved toward him he knew that he was bodiless, that he had never had a body, that what was there would overwhelm them all—Our breath stinks, he said, we're fucked, that fucker knows it.

Beyond this, he would only look at Star-Gazer with a smug and haunted little grin and say, God plays tiddlywinks, and we're the buttons.

Standing here, by the bureau, he winces to think how the boy may have also pored over those few photographs of him that circulate among the Custer crowd: his pale snow-blinded eyes and cherub's lips which seem always pursed to say his own name, *Benteen*. Those dark collars which never seemed to fit around the chewy texture of his neck; the affront of silver hair there at his throat that seemed to sprout up overnight.

A feeling of sorrow comes upon him for the boy who will also come to this. He will know one day, with sudden certainty, that he will never run again.

Here is the best of me, he says to Frabbie, when he brings her one of the blowsy roses he has plucked, so voluptuous they buckle at their centers, nurtured by the fluids from his pan.

Sully asked Burton, every morning, why he spat to either side when he first mounted. And each time Burton smiled sour-toothed and made the same joke, while Scruggs giggled. He said, it keeps the elephants away.

It was the horses they cared for, more than themselves, he remembers, as they urged their great cleft breasts toward the arrows. Martini, behind him at the Washita, muttering soft Italian in his mount's ear. Powell weeping as his horse limped behind him, resting its head on his shoulder every time he stopped, its patient eye against his cheek, until he had to shoot it.

Himself, the only time that he can remember weeping, thinking of it afterward—as if, in this world of just desserts, he caught a glimpse of something else.

The sad privacies of beasts, that they hated to destroy.

Some univeral impulse, maybe.

He has observed Barnes, the groundsman, even as he holds his swelling hand, whispering poor baby, poor little cripple, to the bee that he has crushed.

There was one afternoon a year before the battle.

They had ridden all day through shallow valleys where they came across the spoor of moose and bears. Signs of the Sioux everywhere, in tent poles and damped-down fire beds, although they never saw them. The creeks they crossed were pebbly, and shaded, and filled with an eternity of logs.

They made camp by the river. From where he sat with Star-Gazer and De Rudio, he could see the Choir and Handsome Jack unpacking. Sully pulled the cougar cub out of his jacket, tied a string around its leg, and jerked it when it tried to totter blindly in among the tree roots. Scruggs picked a blister. Simms did a backflip, then squatted down to contemplate his pack.

After they made camp Benteen walked with Star-Gazer

and De Rudio up into the forest, where they came across a mossy clearing. Shsh, De Rudio said, although what disturbed them was the sudden depth of silence. A bird hovered in the sky high above them—Eagle, said Benteen. In the distance they heard Grasshopper Joe sing out a misremembered dance call. De Rudio said, Sometimes we forget it is very beautiful here, I think.

A crashing in the scrub. The smell of urine and of coffee from the camp, followed by the Choir.

Yeah, it's so warm and real, said Handsome Jack who brought up the rear, it's running down my leg.

They saw the Sioux woman at the same time, where she had pulled herself into the low scrub. She had a compound fracture of the left thigh and from the way the blue flesh had pulled back from the bone, and the way she only followed them with her fierce eyes, it was clear she had been there for some time. At the sight of her Simms did two backflips in quick succession, with his mouth agape. Ambrose said, Fish bait—and leaned down to flick her jaw with his toothpick. Before they could take a breath Sully had bent at her throat with the knife and it was done.

Burton sneezed as he opened up her blanket. He looked up to Handsome Jack, who smiled indulgently, then nodded, and gave a mild *Nyow.*

When they had finished, the cub sniffed and chewed sideways on a piece of something. Ambrose the Bilk stamped the woman's pelvis. The bone broke with a low, sudden squeak.

Guess she was a grunter, not a groaner, Handsome Jack said.

⤝⤞

He remembers, now, standing with De Rudio in the meadows out beyond Fort Hays, in the same year as the Washita. Custer had the officers riding in the grass, which was belly-deep on the horses, leaning down to see who could make the biggest bouquets of wild plum and crabapple roses for the ladies. Once he galloped Libbie's name in dark wet capitals across the green. Benteen turned to De Rudio and said, Those wild flowers will not last an hour indoors, even in water, they will wilt.

De Rudio, who already seemed a little stiffer then, shrugged and smiled at him.

They want their *freedom,* they want *life.*

⤝⤞

Lingering here, in the bedroom's calm, he feels a savage urge to go back to the ice house.

Ignoring the scent of stale marrow that pools around his

knees, he will dig beneath the tacky blocks until he finds some grey and granulated bit of muscle; some leathery strip of mammal that can be named no longer; gristle that is drily frozen and unshaped.

He will take this chunk of tissue, wrap it up inside an old piece of cloth, and send it to the boy. He imagines him scattering kittens as he runs and whoops around the room.

He will write:

Having waited these many years for a suitable correspondent, I enclose, with my compliments, this true piece of Custer's heart.

There was a sense, when he was drunk, that every story had its fulcrum; like the flow of water over banks and snags and worn-out clumps of timber; a knowing pulse, a ball-bearing sense of its own weight that it would find in due time in spite of interruptions—*Gotta go drain the donkey, Don't mind if I do, Lord God I'm liquefied*—even his own bitter ramblings would twist in the stream, wait for him to say, *But you know me, I could not keep out of blood,* then turn around and find the middle current.

For Star-Gazer, if he did indeed possess a story of his

own, this shift came during that second-last campaign.

There was a point where, almost overnight, he turned his frail shoulders inward; he grew a preoccupied look that came from somewhere else when they weren't watching, a bright mineral attention in his eye.

That dark and limpid pool of knowledge seemed to well inside him.

Explain to the boy.

The shock was in seeing the Indians as more than an idea. They had grown used to inventing them out of the signs they found, their light tracks upon the snow, the birch bark nibbled by their ponies. The rocks they found sometimes stacked into mute messages in glades where bison flies hung low in cool air above the moss.

There were the prisoners, of course, women and young children, at the forts. And scouts, he guesses, but once they were dressed in army kit he only saw the whiteness in them.

In the last months he saw Star-Gazer sitting near them sometimes, not speaking, his head turned to the side, listening with the parched attention of a crane.

Williams, part-Cree, who tied his scarf into strange tight knots and passed them to the cook's son to untie.

Keen Knife, who liked to shake the soldiers' hands and say his only English words—Okay! Okay! You bet!

Some days Star-Gazer seemed, almost deliberately, to open himself up toward their teasing. His collarbones more ingrown, limp humility about his shoulders. In Montana they collected forage for the horses from beneath the trees; out of the blue Monroe turned toward him. So when do you think you might get out of here, and raise some little Star-Gazers?

He peered out from the depths of his buffalo fur jacket; as if he read a hundred answers on the grey and ragged earth; his smile amused, then suffering, then bashful; the snowflakes fell upon his dry lips.

The corners of his mouth grew slack and weary.

Eventuarily, he said.

There was a part of his soul would always stay out on the plains, Star-Gazer said. It was so frozen he thought a little bit had been torn off.

Odd the scraps they found out on the plains, when they had thought they were the first white men to ride there.

A dog's collar with the buckle still done up.

A child's marble, balanced on a pile of stones beside a bison's track.

A stamp. A steamer ticket.

A rusty brooch with half a cherub carved from lava, impaled upon a twig of sagebrush.

And once, on a river bank, an old cigar, half-smoked and faded, on a patch of sand; the ash still held its ghost-shape, among the dry and quiet tree roots, right down to the band.

Lying on the bed now he can still feel the brusque sweep of Frabbie's hand across the sheets. Her side another country; no hair oil on the pillows, no wadded indentation where she lies.

Tell the boy: who knows if we make history or are made, some impressionable pulp within us held for one brief lifetime by the small simplicities.

Other things inside the bedroom.

The embroidered handkerchief she tied around his jaw when he caught the mumps from Freddie; while she made the knot at the top of his skull she kept her face straight, but when the two edges fell like a rabbit's ears on either side of his head, she began to twitch, then cry, with laughter.

The note he made and put in a shell casing on the morning Freddie delighted them with his first full sentence: *Today will be a blue day*, he said, turning his grey eyes toward them from the doorway.

One night when they were waiting for the first child and she was sick behind the screen he lay in the bed but did not speak, shy suddenly, as if she was a stranger.

You would not go back, he thinks.

When that child died, he had gone out and bought her this pair of earrings, not knowing what to say.

Unbelievable how they scarcely knew each other then; a mystery how anyone might have the faith to gamble on the way a person moved her shoulder, some sympathetic impulse, waiting for the years to do their work.

Dreaming forward, that is how the boy will one day come to see his own life.

Handsome Jack saying, My ring's so polished from all the riding that I could slip it on someone's finger and get myself engaged—

Standing by the Yellowstone, feeling his horse's muzzle in his palm, as tender and insistent as a cunt, the weight of bone and thought behind it—

And then, in a moment, there is Weir, beside him, looking

at the bodies on the battlefield: saying, Oh, how white they look! How white!

$$\times$$

There was a bar in Dakota, run by an old couple they knew only as "the Turkey Buzzards." A book they made you sign, which they liked to sit and read behind the bar. At their bare feet, in the gloom, they had a rag doll for their little dog that they referred to as his "woman," which he would carry about and gnaw then quickly hump. The wife would laugh and say to the dog, I wouldn't want to be your woman, Harry, you're too rough.

$$\times$$

Star-Gazer said when he hit his head on an overhanging bough that he had seen the same strange shapes, wild stars and spirals, that they had found carved into the cave walls in the Black Hills, above the little crested figures, where they had also carved their own names.

He wondered if they were a way of recording pain.

Our fates for the most part, Benteen thinks, are in the things that do not linger.

He has the feeling, suddenly, and it is not unpleasant, that this might be the last day of his life.

When Monroe saw the Bighorn Mountains for the first time, the bracing, piney heft of them, he touched his chest. He said, Oh my mammalian heart.

Pritzker observed, as he held up the oriole's feather, red along its length and grey and tender where it met the under-layer, how much better it would be if we had down instead of pubes.

They knew nothing of Handsome Jack before, he thinks now, except something Star-Gazer had told them, how he'd been too clever for his school up north, and run away.

How little they really told each other of their lives; they did not try, as women do, to make each other less predictable, to rifle in the secret drawers, to find each other out. Instead, each gratefully took over the role assigned, made his language over, offered up his inner longings only as a punchline.

We are the fastidious sex, he thinks.

Something else.

Most of the time, during that last campaign, they barely noticed Custer.

In the cool just after sunset Handsome Jack squatted by the fire with Sully. The night was turning, filled with the chill melancholy of the change of season. Behind them small moths had begun to rise up from the earth.

Sully scratched his chest, then extended his knobby wrists toward the fire bed. He outlined to Handsome Jack the things he had observed during the day about the way that power operates unequally between all men. He hunched and squinted at the stars. He said, chewing with exaggerated thought, Nature is a mother. And, It all comes down to who gets to eat your lunch.

They watched as Burton, panting, lowered his bulk onto the small cushion that he always carried.

Handsome Jack saluted him. Hail Whale!

Scruggs and Ambrose, coming up then, laughed.

Scruggs, you speckled stegosaurus! Ambrose, you old archaeopteryx! said Handsome Jack.

When Maybliss moved for the tobacco pouch, Handsome Jack said,

Bend over, touch your knees
I'll show you what the blind man sees.

He did not seem to expect replies from any of them. He blew a smoke ring, watched absently as Sully bent to readjust the fire.

Handsome Jack had once said the Choir knew each other with the hunched timidity of men who wore bad shoes. Now he had developed some hint of their same posture, something tender and ingrown about him. He had picked up Marshall's way of holding his drink with both hands at his groin and Sully's rapid little underscratch of beard beneath the chin.

Now Burton pulled his huge scrotum from his pants, as was his habit in communal moments. He stretched it outward like a white plate. The others, as they always did, reached out to flick it roughly with their fingers. Hail Whale! they said again as Burton sat back, eyes half-focussed, like a maid daintily holding out the corners of her apron.

Afterward, they continued with their business as if it had not happened; it was the same when Sully suddenly called a name and they all fell upon that person with their fists. Ambrose turned a stick from the fire before his eyes and watched the flame and sometimes gently blew upon it. While Scruggs watched, Maybliss took his collection of coins from his pack and began to spit on them and rub them with a rag. A couple of the quiet, transparent men who had crept to the fringes of the group as it surrounded Burton crept back to their lonely spots again.

Handsome Jack got up and stood against the cliff a little way beyond the Choir. He studied them for some time with his arms folded, and then as he began to stare down at the ground, his face was suddenly quite sober.

De Rudio, who was sitting nearby with Benteen, said, softly, Handsome Jack, would you like to come and share some of our meal?

Handsome Jack jumped, then shot Benteen a quick, wolfish grin.

You're a jewel, he said to De Rudio, who smiled back through the dusk with half-comprehension. If I could find a shop right now I'd buy you the world's gaudiest pocketwatch on a chunky silver chain.

Later Handsome Jack came back with Sully, who grinned and stroked the dark hair that fell at his wrists in silky parts as they stood between Benteen and Monroe. They said, in unison, You're all going cheaper than a tart's breakfast. Then staggered back laughing to their fire.

There is history, he thinks, in punchlines: jokes that could grow ripe in one place only.

Three days before the fighting the rain had brought a host

of frogs out of the mud that jumped into their trouser hems and landed, wetly, on their faces as they lay down in their tents. Something about those cold inner thighs that sickened them. The way they flattened themselves along the tent flaps, the way the men woke to find their clammy fingers in the corners of their mouths.

It was Young Tom who had suggested playing stickball with them. The frogs' smiles had remained benign, even as their bodies stretched like ribbons through the air and exploded on the bat, a sight which made them roar with laughter.

How they had all howled, up on the ridge days later, when Sully hid himself behind a box of crackers and caught the bullet in the mouth that killed him.

And he, he too had laughed.

But why do you tolerate them? Young Tom persisted.

His eyelids sleek and dangerous, Handsome Jack sat like a philosopher with folded arms upon a rock, looking through Young Tom toward the Choir.

Because they have no plans.

Because God has dropped the rule book.

Because they are not ashamed to entertain the small and necessary feelings.

Because, your brother.

Because if nature is a slut, Burton's ass—and here Burton twisted around with a knowing grin—is a big fat dirigible that blocks the lousy view.

Star-Gazer's notebook:

It is a myth to say we are a literal nation. It has never been thus. We are always questing after our own stories; it is the obvious we fear.

To the east the light formed a pale yellowish liquor between the high full moon and the bulky outline of the Bighorn Mountains. They seemed more than ever intent upon the sheer blunt fact of their existence.

The same message, Benteen has thought since, in the bodies the Indians left for them to find, chests peeled back, legs cut to the thigh-bone, filling up with rain.

De Rudio fingered the keys of his trumpet on his lap. The stops made little oily sighs like night birds, but he could not find a tune. At last, further down the camp, Sully put back his head and let out a long sly howl like a coyote and some others joined in chorus. Keogh, beside Benteen, began to talk of holy wells in Ireland littered with broken pottery and bits of rag where you might see a fish and give up the ghost three days later.

The dark also seemed to tilt and lengthen.

De Rudio said, when he was a child his parents used to take him out to look at the shapes of icicles hanging from the trees. The air so cold it got into his bones. This is not an experience, he said, I think a child should have.

On the street outside a man whistles to his dog. It is in among the hydrangeas beneath the window. He can hear the thrash of its belly as it pushes through wet leaves, the low beating of its tail in answer to the man who calls to it again. And now, the eager, meaty weight of it—rump, shoulders, forequarters—as it leaps the fence.

Perhaps, he thinks, it is the noises off that drive us.

His own life shaped as much by the shrill of the Indians' eagle bone whistles and the tickings of the ice house as by his schooling or his marriage.

He sits up straight.

He wants to write the lost thoughts of soldiers.

No, not the grand story, he has never known his life that way, but the seams and spaces in between. This is history too, he thinks, the weight of gathered thoughts, the cumulus of idle moments.

Captain Keogh, for example, with his thick Irish dick, who when he pissed always said that he was making holy water. Young Tom, when he saw it one time, put his hands up to his face and screamed out, in imitation of a pantomime dame, Oh my, a mouse, a mouse!

Pritzker who grew up chewing chicory grindings from the coffee pot, and chewed them still out of his rucksack as he rode; Monroe the cowboy who saw a woman in a field once who had been struck by lightning, the look on her face, he said, was sarcastic, not surprised.

And himself—who knows how much his own temperament was molded by the flat width of the rivers here, the dark mystery of soil, the dogleg tracks?

If you truly wish to understand the battle and my place in it, he writes now to the boy, *you must understand the dreams and jokes and stories that we bore within us. You must see how, as we shared them, they formed a kind of landscape.*

He was the first, that night, to see the woman.

For a long minute, before the others came, she turned her blank and lashless gaze toward him.

Although she had made no sound emerging from the

shadow of the cottonwoods, still they appeared, Handsome Jack and Sully, Custer, Young Tom, the unlisted men, from their fireless camp uphill and gathered by his side; they had sensed this gentle latch within the night that she had slipped through, the white flare of her dress within the dark.

Now this, like war, was the only knowable.

She walked ahead of them, their own backs straightened as they watched hers.

What thoughts their breaths held.

Some warm scent where she had stepped, as secret as the interior of a bird's nest.

He felt Star-Gazer come up beside him, in his greatcoat, and walk behind his elbow. Further ahead he saw Handsome Jack, who had put off his black mood for a moment, turn to Sully with that face of comic concentration he had perfected for when Custer lined them up to give his orders: eyes hazy, his top lip raised and gently quivering. He wondered, for the first time, if Handsome Jack had ever had a woman.

A stitch in the landscape that if they looked at one another would come apart beneath them.

She would not turn until they reached the river.

They walked on, through uneven tree shade, in the night.

For weeks during that last campaign they did not leave the camp. They had grown tired of the gooseberries and cherries growing everywhere, the fertile demands the rising smell of mud seemed to make upon them, the slugs they found, grey and curled like tongues, floating in their cups.

Star-Gazer had not spoken for five days. Instead he slowly examined his knuckles as the rain dripped from the branches of the tree above them.

It might have been Pritzker, Monroe, himself, or any of them, but it was, in the end, De Rudio who stepped up to the silence.

Would you like to see some pornography? De Rudio asked them.

He placed his second and third fingers on his thigh, positioned a blackberry at their apex, and carefully moved the back of a spoon between them so that it mirrored the dark reflection of the cleft.

And they had all smiled then, except Grasshopper Joe who did not get it. And when he did, at last, he fell about with laughter.

De Rudio shoved the spoon into this pocket, as if it was of no importance whatsoever, and began briskly to heat a pot of coffee.

So, he said.

And what of the lost thoughts of Indians, he wonders?

He imagines them, strewn and scattered over all the country, caught randomly among the sagebrush, their own names for the seasons and the secret stitches of their garments as dry and fundamental as the narrow paths worn in the landscape by their feet.

When he'd returned home he gave Evans, who delivers the ice each Monday, one of the Indians' eagle-bone whistles, that he blew for months until he lost it, the high sound through the thin bone as if the ice itself was shrieking.

Star-Gazer: *When feelings reach their highest pitch, they cannot be put in words.*

Look at our photographs, he thinks, and you can see that we carried the idea of the Indians around inside us, big as another continent, just as they carried our love letters and our pocket watches, not for their meaning but the weight of a future yet to be conceived.

The Indians' thoughts lost to us already, from the time that we arrived here.

But out on the plains we were, for the time those wars lasted, linked by our grim geography of fire beds and bullets, in a terrible third nation of our own.

Star-Gazer's theory that the kind of language each country spoke came from the kind of land the people trod on. He wrote, *We have begun to speak slowly and directly.*

Star-Gazer said once, of all the animals on the plains he liked the hares best, the way they crimped in their tails before they ran for the horizon, as if they were embarrassed by the plain and prosy light.

They lay in the shadow of the Bighorn Mountains.

Pritzker said, That cloud hanging there is like a bone, and Monroe shuddered.

Star-Gazer said nothing.

Monroe said, The stars don't keep still, they kind of fidget.

Grasshopper Joe said, The winds from these parts feel as if they come from very far away.

Who was the real Handsome Jack, he wonders now, the one who ran, pushing a pram in which Star-Gazer sat,

cross-legged, along the last mile of the Union Pacific track
—Bender yelling, Bartender! Oh *Bartender*!—before it ran
out into the plains. Or the man he became in those last
weeks, sallow, phlegm beneath the collarbone, who whenever Star-Gazer addressed him would only answer, Have
you ever tickled your tadger with a termite?

We are as the light catches us, he thinks.

A dream Custer had, that he told to Young Tom:

It seemed that he was in another place entirely. He had
lost his color vision, and saw in the vast black and white
expanse before him a fantastic scattering of plugs and
buttes and arches; there was a rock shaped like a gryphon
and another like a long hand that cast a fingered shadow.
The land throbbed with a sleek light that almost had a
heartbeat, that jumped and leaped and popped. And as it
moved toward him he knew that he had never had a body,
that what was there would finish him, and what was there
would also love him. The view jumped, suddenly, with a
tiny flick of shadow as if the sun had eclipsed for a frac-
tion of a second, and then it all changed again before
him—he watched this black and silver light running along
railway tracks, passing under the posts of telegraphs,

touching the edge of a yucca or a cactus, as it spread, like ink, across the land—

It was Star-Gazer who overheard them. Custer in his undershirt, with his braces down around his knees, his voice light and hollow. He shrugged Young Tom off afterward and sat, for a long time, looking out across the plains.

Star-Gazer's strange conviction when he told Benteen, that it was here they might come close to understanding, in the same rudimentary fashion that a man can only touch upon the cold imagination of a spider or a porcupine, something of the inner workings of the man.

Pritzker dreamed he had a porpoise fin, that he said was very sensitive, and covered with his own skin.

Grasshopper Joe saw crowds around an obelisk.

De Rudio said he did not dream, but counted mushrooms in a forest.

There were two little monkeys, Pritzker said, that dipped their paws in a tin of axle grease and sourly rubbed it on the fin.

That same night, Star-Gazer claimed that Pritzker's pelican had stood by his pillow, opened up its fleshy gullet, and dropped a live fish, gasping, in his hat.

As they waited for the dawn, De Rudio played softly on the harmonica he also carried. He said he had put his ear once to a frozen lake, that the high-pitched squeaking of the ice and the movement of the water underneath were quite incredible.

From further down the camp, Handsome Jack called out.

Don't you clusternuts ever go to bed?

They had stopped by a morass for a moment, in order to let the rear catch up. Benteen saw Custer watching his own shadow in the moonlight, his arms folded, shifting his horse so he could throw his shadow even further across the salt-bush and little stacks of rock.

Star-Gazer came up beside Benteen and said, as they heard the steps of the others moving up behind them, his voice soft and flat, untouched by any bitterness, We are from the era of small men.

For some time after the woman disappeared they had looked after her, into the bright dark. No sign of her along the blank edges of the river where the pebbles seemed to draw back mute and silver; no hint of her disinterested passage through the cottonwoods' cold shadow.

Only the sense, in their tight chests, of some door in the night that she had left unlatched. The thought of her long feet, and the white dress clutched before her, as she picked her way beneath the moon's vast light.

Standing there, he remembered an image that had come upon him, walking once, of a town of silences and cobbled streets and long canals that seemed to recognize the passage of his own feet; in which he moved with some impossible directness. He felt, in his own breast, a phlegmy tenderness for all of them.

It is a myth we prove ourselves in war, he thinks: we test ourselves in silence.

The moon low and blazing. The silver river that unravelled in the distance. The terrible stillness of the day caught, where she had lain, in the thin unmoving space above the freezing water.

As they walked back toward the camp, they felt themselves returning to their own dark language.

AT THE TOP OF THE HILL at Little Bighorn, Custer split the troops. When they opened their mouths to speak, or yawn as some did now with fright, they felt the wind rush in to scrub their throats, bringing a scent of the cold red clay of the mountains far beyond them to the south, and the high, spare taste of grass.

He saw Burton the Whale take out the last of his food and eat it quickly.

Monroe, who did not like the feeling of the wind inside his head, tied his kerchief around his mouth.

Grasshopper Joe spat, then looked surprised.

The men gathered behind Custer now and waited. Custer did not seem to see or hear them, as he paced back and forward on his horse, lifted the field glasses and let them fall back on his chest.

Star-Gazer had brought his mount around beside his own. Benteen said, Well I shall see you for a drink next by the Rosebud, and he nodded. Star-Gazer's hands were pale and slack and rested lightly on his saddle. Benteen noticed that he did not wear his glasses, but that he did not seem to squint.

They looked out across the cloud-shadows of the valley. Star-Gazer said that it made him think of a book he had read once about the cold places of the deep.

Then Handsome Jack rode up and thrust his mount between Star-Gazer's and Benteen's. He had shaved off the beard that he had let grow in pubic majesty throughout the whole campaign. His face was radiant and spiteless, filled with queasy benediction.

He said to Star-Gazer, I thought you only read children's books.

Something surfacing between the two of them again, as dark and fragile as the vein inside a shrimp. Star-Gazer looked at him and blinked, his lips dry and slack, in that slow way he had before he came up with a joke, as if he was at a loss for what to say.

He said, actually, it was a picture book. His favorite in the Junior Readers' series.

The sun went cold behind a cloud. Their horses, fighting hard against the reins, tried to crop the grass. Pritzker, his mount pacing nervously, pulled up momentarily behind them. He said he had a fancy, once this campaign was done, that he might quit, buy a cart and open up his own stall in a city, selling apples or canaries.

Nibblenuts to that, Handsome Jack said, and curled his lip into a manic grimace. I'm planning to become a child genius myself.

Star-Gazer said, his face inscrutable as Custer gave the signal, I'm still waiting to be born.

As one he and Handsome Jack nimbly turned their horses' heads and took off downhill, after Custer, side by side.

Those two days on the ridge, standing tall, untouched by bullets, he had felt his life stretch out, cool and perfect as the bolts of cloth he had once watched unfurling from a train wreck in the desert.

During that long night, the dead and dying all around him, he had imagined it settling soft and cold upon the dirt, and that they also felt its shelter. Lying there, his cheek against his rifle, not knowing that the others were already dead, he imagined the tender gathering of moths or frogs before them in the places where they lay.

Afterward, standing with Captain Weir among the bodies, trying to identify a hat or button—nothing to be found of Star-Gazer but those notebooks.

Those remains of Monroe that they bound up in his kerchief. Which bobbed like meaty testicles from the saddle at his knee.

And now from down the river, he hears the church bells ring. Soon Frabbie will be here and she will put her hands, cool from touching hymn books, on his head.

Strange, when they came across the bodies, how he had remembered the one time, many years before the battle, that Handsome Jack had come here with him on leave; Frabbie out of town with Freddie, visiting her sister. Handsome Jack started and stepped back when he saw the bumps the damp had made beneath the paper of the hallway; turning and smiling weakly at Benteen. His face grey and freshly shaved, he backed against the stair rail. The drink clutched in both his hands, as if living in a house was something you might catch.

He could not look at the coat-rack. Some indelicate hint of Frabbie and the child in the jackets, that made him move with fleshy tenderness, his rear tucked tight, his eyes cast down, as if his toenails pained him.

Each time their gazes met he nodded curtly at Benteen, then raised the glass and grinned. His hands shook. He peered with great exaggeration at the walls, then flicked them with his fingers.

He asked, Don't you have a little priest hole?

He forced a trembling leer, as if they both knew a hallway was a smutty joke.

Benteen, playing along, his face grave, said he was afraid that they did not.

Then I simply can't stay, Handsome Jack had said.

And walked back toward the edge of town, his chin held high, his thighs stiff, into the greying light.

He wonders now if Frabbie has ever had regrets. Speaking for himself, he has none, except they are for her.

Years afterward, in their quarters, they had been arguing over something when Frabbie had stepped back into the kettle and knocked its scalding water down her thighs. She had gasped, then stood there still and soaking. Without thinking, he had put her over his knee and stripped the steaming under-garments from her; grabbing the cook's honey from the pantry he had poured the whole pot on the burn.

In bed, three days later, he felt the blister burst against his hip; the liquid hot then cooling; the sweetness of the honey soaking him, mixed with the pale internal fluids of her skin. He had been startled into sudden rut then, like an old stallion, at the thought of her cool buttocks on his lap.

He is too humble, suddenly, for history this morning. If he truly wishes to understand the battle and his place in it, he writes to the boy, he thinks he will find everything he requires in this one document.

He attaches Handsome Jack's list of farts:

The geyser, titmouse, beard-splitter, silent angel, granny; teacher's breath, the virgin's sneeze; the schoolgirl's friend, the undertaker's mate; blanket-lifter, mudslide, shotgun wedding; dead man walking; hobo, the child molester, pistols at dawn; power of attorney, the second coming, Revelations.

For some months he has been troubled by the memory of his mother, when he was quite a young man, and they stood, near the shaded river, by her spaniel's grave.

She said, That dog was the love of my life, and her tired face was lit up with a sudden tenderness.

He felt keenly all her sex's injuries in that one sentence. And seemed, at the same time, to sustain some mysterious damage of his own.

And now he thinks, suddenly, that there is no more important detail he can tell the boy about those two days pinned
down on the ridge, than that they had to scramble in their
packs to find their mess kits, and dig out their positions there
with spoons and forks.

In a moment Frabbie will be home. If he were to describe
Frabbie to the boy, it would be as he has always imagined
her, as an archaeologist, collecting pots in some cold
desert.

Sometimes, in the early years, she would slowly move
herself across his hips, her face serious, and take his seed
inside her like a thought. At other times, the hot gift of her
insides opened up as she lay beneath him, she would draw it
from him swiftly with her cries.

He imagines Frabbie as she lays him out upon the parlor
table, his jacket with its brevet ranking on the sideboard; she
folds his hands together and unshucks his penis like a mollusk, wipes it briefly with the cloth.

Outside, there is a ripple in the water. Some cold knowledge in it, as he feels it pass beyond the window, past the birds' nests and low willows on the muddy banks, the houses with their cool flagging, and the tallow works.

When Freddie was little and they stood there by the river he would say, That squirrel moves as if it has its coat on, that cat has made its boat shape.

Oh Frabbie, he would like to say to her, you have relieved me of my language.

Sometimes he has a letter from De Rudio, who lives in a monastery in Germany, where there are benches in the grounds for the monks to sell their sweet beer with sausages and dumplings, where you must walk to the bottom of a cliff face and cross the swift pale river on a punt. He writes, *There was a degustation, and I did it.* Or, *Here it is becoming cold and the trees change their dresses.*

I often think if you would come here I would have to show you some things and talk funny English to you. I am writing a piece for the musicians—I will put the right note in the right place, and I love to do this, but it is not a short work and after I am gone I hope they make it fine.

At the table now he gathers it all up—the jottings, the lists, the pages from Star-Gazer's notebook, his starts at letters— and makes a thick package for the boy.

He slips in a note,

Sir, It was my intention to render an account of my life, as honest as I could make it, and found that I could not. Instead, it is my honor to forward on these fragments in which you will find us as we were. Treat us kindly—or not, perhaps. As we deserve.

Take care of those cats,

Your friend, Brevt. Brigadier General Frederick W. Benteen

He smiles as he thinks of adding as a postscript—*I believe no thing has brought me such uncomplicated pleasure as the eager shapes of ducks.*

Outside, the bright sheen of the river passing and repassing.

For a moment he is back out on the plains, the cloud-shadow moving like a flattened ocean, the swells repeated in the muscles of the horses, an edgeless universe of grass.

When Frabbie returns he will call Aulda, the maid, to take a small tool from the pantry and shave a spray off one of the blocks out in the ice shed.

She will bring it to them in the study; no water, no whiskey, in the glasses, he wants to taste the New England pond-juice. Frabbie, with her stockinged feet up on the foot-stool, will sip the drink as if she accepts quietly everything that floats within it.

And he will lean in, and look into her eyes to say, You know that I have always loved you, then squeeze her toe instead.

Frabbie will study him for a moment, as if she tucks the thought away.

It's geography they're drinking, he will tell her, the con-fluence of streams, a precise concentration of suspended peat and weed and superficial flora.

While not intended as a realist narrative, *The Lost Thoughts of Soldiers* is based on an historical incident and its aftermath.

Brevet Brigadier General Frederick W. Benteen was a Captain in the Seventh Cavalry at the time of the Battle at Little Bighorn. I am indebted to Charles K. Mills's biography of Benteen, *Harvest of Barren Regrets*, and John M. Carroll's *Camp Talk*, a collection of letters from Benteen to his wife Catharine "Frabbie" Benteen for a number of details. Benteen and Frabbie bore five children, none of whom survived infancy except Freddie, born in 1867. While this novel places Benteen in a home built by his father in Georgia, he was actually born in Virginia, and only settled in Atlanta with Frabbie (who, in reality, moved between army quarters with Benteen) at the end of his career.

The name "De Rudio" will sound familiar to some readers: I have adapted the name of 2nd Lieutenant Charles C. DeRudio, who joined the Seventh in 1869, for my fictional bugler. I have also borrowed the nicknames "Star-Gazer" and

"Handsome Jack" after coming across them in a list of soldiers who had served with the Seventh. Captain Weir's exclamation, "Oh how white they look! How white!" on seeing the bodies on the Little Bighorn battlefield is taken from Edward S. Godfrey's eyewitness account of the aftermath. The Whittaker biography referred to by Benteen is Frederick A. Whittaker's *A Complete Life of General George A. Custer*, written (with the assistance of Libbie Custer) and published in 1876, the same year as the battle.

In 1879, President Hayes ordered a Court of Inquiry into Major Marcus Reno's conduct at Little Bighorn. Opinion is still divided on whether Reno was hysterical, but guarded testimony suggests that he did not fight well that day, although he was cleared. Benteen's cool behavior was universally praised, and he was credited by most for taking command of Reno's shattered troops on the bluff after their retreat. Benteen received official notification of his promotion to Major in 1883, and was finally brevetted to Brigadier General in 1890. He continued to serve until 1888, when, having faced a court-martial in Fort Duchesne, Utah, for drunkenness, he was granted a medical discharge. He died in Atlanta in 1898.

Debate rages to this day over whether Benteen ought to have—or indeed could have—obeyed Custer's note to "Bring Pacs."

It appears that spelling for the Little Bighorn was not standardized at the time of the battle: on maps and in documents

"Bighorn" and "Big Horn" appear to be interchangeable. For consistency, I have chosen to follow the spelling used by the Little Bighorn National Monument in Montana.

D.H. Lawrence's description of a Zeppelin attack is taken from a letter to Lady Ottoline Morrell (as quoted in Douglas Botting, *Dr Eckener's Dream Machine: The Great Zeppelin and the Dawn of Air Travel*).

My heartfelt thanks to the following people for reading and commenting on this draft at different stages: Richard Harling, Simeon Barlow, Peter Bishop, Malcolm Knox, Nikki Christer, Fran Bryson and Judith Lukin-Amundsen. Thanks to the Burgesses and N. Bender for your hospitality in Wyoming; the Nubs for lupabrilles; Norbert Vollath and Berit Hüttinger; Tim Smith for this schooldays; and James Bradley for the dinosaur. Thanks also to the following for grants and residencies that assisted with the writing of this book: the Marten Bequest, the Faculty of Arts at the University of Wollongong, the Australia Council, and Bundanon Artists' Centre.